Shadow to Sunshine

CATHLEEN ELLIS

MONTANA
IOWA
COLORADO
KANSAS
GEORGIA

Other Books by Cathleen Ellis

www.CathleenEllis.com

A Scarf of Promise

Castle in the Air

Making Our Way

Kara's Love

Baskets on Christmas Lane

Up to Me

Christmas Bright

A Voice for Gabby

Love Ties

Roses for Meredith

Old Crooked Road

Just Let It Go

Tend My Flowers

Together Now

Sky Tossed

A Humble Task

What's Beneath

Loving Presence

1

August 1992

"My year's up, and I gotta rejoin my special ops group. Cassie, you gonna be OK?"

"Course, Dad, we been doin' so good together, this past year. I know I must be with family, and we been plannin' this for several months."

"It's somethin' I been wanting to do for a long time. And with you going to be with Grandma Maggie, that can happen. Cassie, we've moved from shadow to sunshine. I'm very grateful to you, my wonderful daughter."

Jeff Montclare hugged her, as she put her arms around him and patted his back.

She stepped away from him and grinned, "We're talking about our dreams. You'll get to do yours, and before long, I'll get to do mine. We're Army strong."

"Roger that, sweet girl."

They smiled and gave each other a crisp salute.

"GMag needs me, I'm 14, 15 soon, got a solid head on my shoulders. You tell me that."

Cassie saw tears spring to his eyes. That started her tears. As she stood there with her dad her mind reeled back over the last two years. Her Granddad Montclare died, leaving the veterinary practice to his veterinarian wife, Maggie. Then, unbelievably, last year, in August the brain tumor that killed her granddad was the same kind of tumor that took her mom, Isabella, from her husband and daughter.

Jeff and Cassie held hands as they walked through the clean and empty tri-plex where they lived since Isabella died.

"Best thing we did, Cassie, sold or donated most of the furniture when we left the house. Downsizing came hard, but we did it. And now, you've got your belongings, your bike, bed, dresser, desk, and books on the way to Ephrine."

"Dad, what about your stuff?"

"Just a few things, sent on to grandma's, like yours. I just don't know exactly where I'll be based for the next couple of years, 'til you graduate. I'll find housing wherever I'm sent."

"Dad, you'll be TDY a lot."

"Exactly."

They let go of each other's hands as Jeff locked the front door. Another military family would take possession of that on-base housing that afternoon. They moved down the walkway from the tri-plex, then turned and gave their place one last look.

"How many homes, Dad, since I was born?"

"Uh, let's see, with this place," he paused for a moment to count, "at least 10, in the US and Germany and England."

"You weren't with us, for part of that time."

"Right, my jobs kept me away from the two most precious people in my world."

They spent the night in guest housing at the Army base half way to their destination. By late afternoon of the next day they drove to the home in Ephrine, Georgia, where Jeff lived with his parents since he was 11. Cassie hurried to the front porch and rang the doorbell. She waited a bit, then waved to her dad. He walked into the back yard and found the hidden key which his folks kept on the inner part of the wood fence since he was a teenager. Cassie proceeded to bring the suitcase, satchels and boxes from the SUV up to the front porch. The final item was a thin but heavy rectangular box which her dad carried in.

Cassie read the note taped on the refrigerator door handle.

Welcome Cassie and Jeff. I'm excited to see you and hope to be home by 6 p.m. barring any emergencies. Your goods arrived yesterday (that was fast) so I had the movers put your furniture in your room, Cassie. Jeff, your stuff's in the basement bedroom. We'll figure out where to store it. Covering for the new vet to our practice. He's taking a well-deserved weekend (three days).

Jeff looked around. He barely recognized the home he knew since his preteen days. He heard his daughter rummaging in her upstairs bedroom.

"Dad, the movers already put my bed stuff on top of the frame," she hollered from the top of the stairs.

Jeff brought up a box of Cassie's stuff and returned for another satchel. She carried up the suitcase she used for several years when she visited her grandparents.

He stood and looked around at her room.

"Wow, Grandma's made some mighty serious changes around here. Do you like the color?"

"Uh huh, GMag asked me what color I wanted my room. I told her, and here it is."

"Lovely color, Cassie, soothing, the pale lavender."

"Dad, you weren't here last summer, but GMag redid nearly the whole house. Looks nuthin' like what Granddad lived with."

"Yeah, I like it; she decluttered."

"We took twenty or so trips to the donation centers during the time I was here."

"She musta taken time off."

"She did, we shopped a little, and she took me to Savannah for great food and to see the beautiful homes. I'll help her at the clinic 'til school starts, that's in just a few days."

"Good, sounds like you got everything worked out."

He saw his daughter's smile. He felt the sting of tears in his eyes as he thought about her losing two important people in her life, one after the other.

"You seem happy, Cassie."

She came to him and gave him her wide grin.

"I'm lots better, I'll have sad times, but God loves me and I love him. He'll take care of me, besides GMag and you."

He hugged her and kissed her on top of her blonde head.

"Grandma has a mattress pad, sheets, pillowcases, and bedspread all nice and washed, waiting for me."

"Let me help you make up your bed."

Cassie teamed with her dad, fixing the bed up in quick time.

"I gotta take care of my stuff; you go ahead and unpack."

"Thanks for your help with the bed; it'll never get made that fast again, Dad."

They laughed as they high fived each other.

ℴℴ

Jeff grilled steaks, Cassie fixed the lettuce and veggie salad, and Maggie baked the potatoes in the microwave.

"Busy Friday, Mom?"

"Frustrating, a couple of owners who did not follow through with the instructions I gave them about the meds for their dogs."

"So, the dogs were back for a second visit?"

"Right, I love the animals I work with, the humans," she paused and shook her blonde hair to them, "sometimes not so much."

She stuck out her tongue.

Cassie and Jeff laughed with Maggie. They ate dinner together on the screened-in back porch. Afterward, before dessert Jeff wanted to share with his family.

"So, I'll tell you the banner story, what I know. I'd like you to follow through with this, Cassie, you're old enough now, and I know you like searching for answers to serious questions, like cures for TB and the auto immune stuff, that's fascinated you for years."

Cassie helped Jeff unfold the banner from the box and place it across the wood floor of the great room.

"Dad, your granddad, had this in his possession for a long time. He's wanted to return it to its rightful owner, but he doesn't know who that is. He told me as his condition worsened that he wouldn't have time to research, so he gave the task to me. And I'm handing it over to you. It's kinda a mystery, what does the banner represent, where did it come from? Dad never shared with me. See here in the bottom corner, a piece of material's been torn away along with the fringe."

He turned a section of the banner over. Cassie saw a small and withered piece of paper, attached to a corner of the two-sided banner with two rusty straight pins.

She read the small scrawling penmanship, "September 192 ." Cassie shook her head, "Whew, can't read the last number."

Then she spoke out, "Return to and the rest of the ink wording smeared together, it's unreadable."

"Clues, I guess?" Jeff spoke to his mom.

Her grandma sat near them on a footstool.

"Granddad never shared any of this with me. I didn't even know the banner existed until right now. It was between granddad and your dad. But, Cassie, I can work with you, about when granddad was younger, if that'll help."

Maggie walked around the banner, counting her steps as she went length, then width.

"Good sized, can tell it might have been carried on a pole, with these insets on the left side. It probably was a nice color, maybe a medium purple. And the wording, Hawks, is in a nice flowing print. This cost a lot, back in the day, like the piece of paper says, 1920 something. I'd say it belonged, uh, to a college or university, perhaps to a band or an athletic team. And," Maggie paused as she knelt down near the top of the banner, "up here at the top right, on both sides, it says

Cooper's, in tiny print." Maybe the school had a mascot of Cooper's hawks."

"For sure, Dad and GMag, it needs to be returned to its rightful owner. It sure shouldn't be thrown away."

"So, my daughter, do you have a plan for solving this mystery?"

She gave her dad a studied look, her forehead creasing as she thought. She didn't speak for a couple of minutes. Then she nodded her head.

"I do," she paused, "for starters; I'll take pictures of the banner, lay it out in the backyard. I'll do a couple of shots out the window of my bedroom. It looks directly out at the back yard. You know the nice 35 mm. camera you and mom got me when I was 11?"

"Uh huh."

"I'll also get some closer up ones, standing on a ladder and looking down at the banner. Then I'll get the film developed and have copies made; on the roll I've already got a couple pictures from the end of last school year with my friends."

Cassie moved closer to her grandma.

"GMag, I'll go to the Ephrine library one morning next week, before I come in to help. I'll start researching universities that were around this area in the 1920's. My thought is that the banner is from a school in this area," she paused, and nodded, "here in the South."

"That's great, Cassie, for you to start work on this project, helping your granddad and dad."

"Remember Grandma, I kinda have a clue, granddad graduated from the University of Georgia, and from vet school at Auburn University."

"Let's take a break, Mom, and have dessert. Then Cassie and I'll fold the banner and return it to the box."

Maggie fixed them each a dessert plate of a large brownie and dip of vanilla ice cream, all slathered with chocolate sauce. Along with that she made decaf coffee.

"GMag, so delicious, yummy."

"This's special; ice cream alone is our usual dessert, unless you want to bake something to go with it."

"Yeah, I can do chocolate chip bars."

"Mom, I attest to the deliciousness of Cassie's chocolate chip bars."

"You're hired, young lady," Maggie giggled to Cassie as she touched her granddaughter's shoulder.

"We're gonna get along fine, just like last summer."

Cassie put her spoon down and leaned over to hug her grandma.

"Thanks, I love my new sheets, pillow cases and bedspread. My stuff," she shook her head, "stuff from my old princess and butterfly days, time to give away."

"After we clean up from dessert and put the banner away, we need to talk about Cassie's sophomore year. Jeff, this'll be a slight change from what you and I talked about earlier this summer."

"Whatever you and Cassie decide, Mom."

As they worked together to fold the banner for placement back in the box, Cassie spoke up, "I want to talk to Father Paul again. He listened to my crying, to my sad words last summer. To tell the truth, I'm still feeling pretty bad sometimes, missing mom."

"Sweet pea, we'll get back to seeing Father. I need to go with you. I'm missing your granddad a lot at times, especially when things get stressful at work."

She paused and looked directly at her son.

"He calmed me, Jeff, your dad did."

"I know that, Mom. Are you still in touch with your two friends?"

"Only one now, since he died. I feel kinda abandoned."

Cassie spoke up then, "Tell her, Dad."

"Yeah, the couples that used to be a part of our lives, now that Isabella is gone, not one of them still gets in touch with me. I've made new friends, folks who understand the sadness, the anger I feel in losing a loved one."

"Oh my goodness maybe that happens to all folks who lose someone they love, do you think, Jeff and Cassie?"

"Yeah, GMag, you may be right. I'm glad I had only two close friends at Smith High. They stayed loyal to me, by my side, they honored the tears I shed, they cried too, like I was sharing my grief with them."

Jeff came to Maggie and Cassie as they stood together. The three of them hugged as their tears came.

"I feel them still with us," Jeff choked as he spoke through his tears.

Cassie stepped away from her dad and grandma. She looked into their tearful eyes with her own, her tears still falling on her cheeks.

"They're in my heart," Cassie put her hand over her heart, "staying in my memory too."

Her family nodded to her, and though their faces held tears, she saw their smiles.

Cassie and her dad said their goodbyes that night. And Jeff left at 5 a.m. the next morning. Maggie got up to see him off.

"I'm usually up about this time; I make coffee and do chores about the home, pretty tuckered out when I get home in the evening. I'm glad we're all three in agreement about Cassie's school."

They sat together, sipping coffee.

"I'll be in touch, as I can be. Cassie's an outstanding student; she'll make you proud, Mom, as she always has her mom and me."

"Got it, son, go forward with your dreams."

They hugged as he whispered to her, "I love you Mom, thank you for everything, my life."

"I love you. God speed, Jeff."

හ

"Cassie," her grandma knocked on her bedroom door, "I'm off to the clinic. I want you to chill this morning and get yourself settled in. Come to the clinic about 1 p.m. I'll have a break then and we'll go to our favorite little café nearby."

"See you then, GMag," Cassie spoke out in a groggy voice, "I'm sending you a hug."

"Hey, I can feel it and I'll see you soon."

"Bye Grandma, I love you."

"And I love you."

Cassie slept in for a little while. She heard the songbirds chirping their tunes in the backyard. That prompted her to get up. She showered, dressed and headed downstairs to the kitchen. Her grandma stayed with the same routine they had last summer. Maggie listed the tasks to be completed for that Saturday. She also put down the major things they needed to accomplish for the entire next week. That way, she could spend a little time away from the clinic with her granddaughter before Cassie started school.

She fixed herself scrambled eggs and toast. There was just enough coffee left in the pot for her to have one cup. She remembered her grandma's advice, "For every cup of coffee, please drink a cup of milk. You're still a growing kid."

So she reversed the drinks and had the milk first, then the hot coffee.

"Ever since mom died, coffee's been a comfort, its warmth, helping me remember mom. She loved coffee and drank a lot of it," Cassie spoke out as she finished up the cup and took her dishes to the sink.

After she cleaned up, she looked again at the week's list her grandma kept on the side of the refrigerator.

"Whew, it's gonna be a busy Saturday," she nodded her head as she finished unpacking and arranging her room.

She unfolded the boxes and put her suitcase, satchels and the boxes in the basement closet. She slid the box containing the banner under her bed. Two bathrooms were next on her cleaning chore list. Her grandma cleaned her own bathroom off the master bedroom. Cassie gathered her dirty clothes combining her grandma's washing to her own. After she added detergent, she started the washer. Cassie glanced at the hamper that sat in the laundry room, for grandma's work outfits, including ones that had blood on them. Her grandma insisted on doing that wash herself using a lot of colorfast bleach along with the laundry detergent. She asked Cassie never to mix those work outfits with their personal laundry.

After she finished the clothes drying, Cassie stepped out in the back yard.

"Don't know how you do it, GMag, with your job, you still have these gorgeous roses every summer."

She leaned down and took a deep breath, smelling the tangy odor of the bright orange rose.

"Wow, it's gotta be over four feet tall," she whistled out.

Opening the side gate she moved to the front yard. Her grandma kept the front yard landscape simple, with grass and several small bushes close to the house. One tree stood in the middle of the yard. Cassie looked the small tree over and inspected the leaves.

"Not sure you're gonna make it, little guy."

Cassie remembered last August when the arborist told them the big oak had to come down; diseased was the diagnosis. She stood, feeling sad, watching from a safe distance as the tree service cut down the beautiful 20 foot tree.

"It was such a great tree; I had my tree swing, and I used to swing high," she recalled telling her grandma.

"Honey, the arborist felt like it was a hazard, could fall on our home in a big wind. Our neighbor two doors down lost a big guy like this one in a microburst a couple of years ago, not going to take any chances."

Cassie shook her head at the remembrance. She left the little tree and returned to the backyard.

"I know grandma will let me mow this year. She's been doing all the work herself. I can sure help; then in October we'll have leaves for two months."

She checked the kitchen clock time and picked up the house key which she added to her key ring. She headed to meet her grandma for late lunch and to spend time shopping.

"So beautiful, these all are," Cassie spoke out as she strode down the streets of her Grandma's area, seeing the stately homes and trees, built after WWII. She noticed the renovations on many homes. She walked the three blocks to the Montclare Animal Clinic on Main Street.

"Hey Cassie, how are you?"

"Quite content; glad I'm here," she smiled to Kay Ann, the vet tech, as they hugged.

Cassie hugged Analease, the vet tech for the new vet.

"We're sure happy to have your help for the next few days. There's always a push before school starts here, almost like the animals are heading off to school like the kids are."

Miriam, the receptionist and bookkeeper, finished her phone call and came around the front of the desk to hug Cassie.

"My, my, young lady, you continue to grow taller. It's good to see you."

After their hug, Cassie stepped back from Miriam.

"Yeah, I'm glad to be back."

"And how did Smith High School treat you?"

"I learned a lot, and I studied hard."

Cassie heard clapping and saw smiles, from the ladies and her grandma, who just came into her sight.

Maggie stood next to her granddaughter and hugged her shoulder.

"See you ladies on Monday. Brad'll be back."

The women nodded. On Saturdays the helpers left the clinic at 2 p.m. Sunday was their only full day off. Cassie and her grandma walked down the street to a favorite lunch spot.

They ordered immediately, both knowing what they wanted for lunch. Cassie drank part of her soft drink, then switched to water.

"You first, GMag, how'd it go this morning?"

"Filled with animals that needed inoculations and tags, for all the folks who work Monday through Friday. Saturdays are a great partial day to be open; we're always super busy.   And what about you, my beautiful granddaughter?"

Maggie paused, smiling to Cassie, "And getting more so every day."

Cassie felt a blush rise from her throat to the top of her head.

"Yeah, room in order, showered and made breakfast, bathrooms cleanup, and washed and dried a load of clothes, mostly mine."

Her grandma gave her the look.

"And," she nodded to Maggie, "I didn't touch your work clothes. You taught me well."

"Chow down, Cassie."

"Dessert?"

"Course."

They finished their hamburgers and fries and ordered warm cherry pie with ice cream.

"Well, how does your school sound to you, Cassie, now that you've had a little time to absorb what we think is best for you?"

Cassie nodded, "So grateful for you and dad to think of my academic career, but, GMag, Hillyer, wow, so expensive."

"You're not to be concerned; your dad's got everything under control. It's your mom's life insurance; she wanted what your dad wants, the best education possible for you. You'll be squared away, through the next three years and your entire college education. Grad school may be a little dicey, but that's a ways from now."

"You're sure, Grandma?"

"I expect you not to worry; your academics are critically important. What we wish for you is that you learn all you can and have fun in the process."

Maggie took Cassie's hand and squeezed it with her own as she smiled to her granddaughter.

ℰꝋ

"This'll be quick, Cassie."

She smiled to her grandma as they and the sales lady collected her clothes for school.

"This red blazer fits great; the lady says I need a lightweight one and a winter blazer?"

"Right, and light weight and heavier weight red and black plaid pleated skirts, winters here can be cold. That's why you have both long and short sleeve white shirts, for the temp variation. I'll teach you how to tie your black tie. Some days you all will be really dressed up, so the tie. Other times you'll have open collars."

"There's a calendar, of what outfits we wear on which days?"

"There is, one of the discipline requirements of attending Hillyer."

Cassie put on her entire outfit, complete with her nearly knee high black socks. She slid into her new black loafers, one of the acceptable shoes according to the uniform code.

"Well, it's like my folks, they were always in uniform, getting ready for work. It's just the same for me, except mine is a school uniform."

They carried the bags with her new uniforms and shoes to Maggie's van.

"Exactly, Cassie, that's a good way to look at your school situation. Right away the administration knows who is, and who is not going to fit in to this mighty fine school you'll be attending."

"It'll be a thousand degrees of difference, from Smith High School last year. But that's OK. I'm preparing for the university, and Hillyer will help me do that."

ℰꝋ

"Father Paul, I'm back, this time 'til I graduate."

Cassie shook hands with Father outside after the church service at St. Luke.

"I'm glad to see you; you may want to visit me with your grandma."

"I'll make an appointment with the church secretary. Yes, I need to talk with you again, Grandma'll come too. We still grieve."

Father nodded his head and put his other hand over Cassie's.

"Take care, Father."

"You folks, also."

Cassie and GMag headed straight for the cemetery. They were both anxious to go to the graves of Dr. Stephen Montclare and Major Isabella Birmingham Montclare.

They each carried a rose from the Montclare garden. They held hands as they approached the graves.

"Gosh, it's been since last summer, Grandma, I'm glad we came. It'll be my first time seeing mom's gravestone."

She left her grandma and knelt in the grass at her mom's grave. Cassie whispered, "I'm with you now, Mom, where you rest. But know that your spirit resides in my heart. One thing for sure, God's with me, always. It's a comfort to never be alone. I'll make you proud of me this year. Me and grandma, what a team we make."

She placed a single long-stemmed yellow rose on the ground in front of her mom's gravestone.

"Miss you, Mom," she choked as the tears came and her nose mucous drained down the back of her throat. She sat on the backs of her shoes and put her hands together in prayer.

"I'm starting to forget what you look like. So I have your military uniform picture in a frame next to my bed. And next to that I have my favorite picture of you and dad, horsing around in the back yard of our home at Fort Bragg. That's right before you got so sick. It's a picture I took myself with my special camera. GMag and me, we'll be back to visit."

Cassie stood and looked up at the blue-green sky with a ruffle of white clouds off to the east. She shook her head and wiped away her tears with a tissue. She turned to see her grandma standing, with her hand on the top of her granddad's gravestone.   GMag's lips moved, but she spoke nothing out loud.   Cassie saw that she placed the long-stemmed red rose in front of her husband's gravestone.

The rest of that day Cassie read in her room, and her grandma read in hers. They both rested, from the flurry of activities of the last few days. That evening they dressed up and went out to dinner at a favorite restaurant of Maggie's. Together they celebrated the lives of Steph and Isabella.

℥

Kay Ann asked Cassie to help with the dog.

"Pick up on this dog's at 11 a.m. He'll wear the plastic collar at home until the stitches heal. He'll be back to have them removed from his back leg. Oh, I see a family member's already here."

Cassie helped the dog owner's son by carrying the meds and extra bandages to the pickup. The young man lifted the dog to the passenger side of the front seat. Cassie handed him the supplies the family would need for the dog's care.

"Hey thanks, for your help with Dover. You're an outstanding hottie."

He nodded his head, and she watched him give her a heated, bright-eyed look.

"I should screw you, right here and now," he started to smile to her.

Cassie slapped him as hard as she could. She saw the instant redness on his cheek and the stunned surprise in his eyes. She turned around and walked fast down the street to the clinic. Cassie did not look back.

She felt her face flush bright red. Tears came to her eyes.

"What an unbelievable jerk," she repeated it to herself over and over again.

When she got control of her temper, she checked in with Miriam and found out the family name and the name of the jerk.

That Monday evening Cassie made dinner. She fixed one of her favorites, soft tacos and refried beans. They decided to eat inside, because they knew that outside the hot and sticky Georgia summer kept up its relentless heat.

"If we get that rain shower they promised us, we'll have dessert on the back porch. What'cha think?"

"Sounds great, GMag."

The showers did come. They sat down at a table in the screened back porch with their dessert, cheese cake. An easy breeze cooled them as they ate.

"Grandma, I gotta share somethin' with you." Her voice started to waver. "I wrote out what happened. I'm so upset."

Cassie handed the handwritten statement to her. Her grandma read through the information, twice. She set the page down and drank the rest of her coffee.

"I'm so sorry, Cassie, that this's happened to you. I know this family, especially the father. I will contact him tomorrow and share this with him. That kind of behavior cannot occur, not in my clinic, or with my employees, and most especially, not toward you."

Cassie started to cry. Her grandma came around and hugged Cassie where she sat.

"Everything's been going so good for me. This's set me back; I wish dad were here."

Maggie moved her chair next to Cassie's.

"No honey, I don't think you really mean that. Remember, your dad is a trained killer. He also can be a gentle man, that is the way you know him. Better that we say a prayer, right now."

Cassie began, "God, I forgive this incredible piece of shit for his sexist, derogatory comment to me."

"Cassie, try again."

She started to cry, then thought to herself, "Whoever this kid is, he's not worth my time or effort to get upset over, I gotta move on."

She took a deep breath, "God, I forgive this young man for his comment to me."

"That's better."

They sat together for a little while, Maggie holding Cassie's hand.

"God," Maggie began, "please forgive him for his unbelievable choice of words directed to my granddaughter."

The next afternoon at 2 p.m. Maggie asked Cassie to meet her in the small office Maggie sometimes used to talk to the animal owners.

"Cassie, this is Reverend Michael Sjarlendone, and his son, Ian."

Cassie nodded to the minister. She averted her eyes from the son.

"Cassie, I am incredibly stupid, making that sexual remark to you. I let my hormone-addled brain get the best of me. I sincerely apologize, and please accept my letter of apology."

She moved her eyes to his hand and took the letter from him. She opened the letter and read it slow, once, and a second time. Then she nodded her head twice to the father as she gave him eye contact.

Her grandma led the father and son from the room and asked them to leave the clinic. Then she returned to Cassie after she closed the door.

"I'm so sorry, Cassie, there are boys out there who will care for you, for who you are, and not just for the way you look. Your dad and I love you, cherish you so much. God loves you and you love him."

"Sometimes Grandma, it's really hard to be an attractive person; you were a stunner when you were younger, uh you still are beautiful. Was it hard for you?"

"Very, especially in vet school, back then there weren't many females in the program. I developed a thick skin, but I confronted the stupid guys. They left me alone after that. And it was tough for me with other women, petty jealousies. I know you'll make friends. I have you signed up for dance class on Saturdays."

"Wow, that's great, thanks Grandma; it was such fun last summer. Maybe some of those girls will be back for this dance year. I met two girls I really liked."

She gave her grandma a wide smile.

"I imagine they'll be back in class; we have a batch of serious dancers in our community. You're to the point now where you'll be in competitions, and possibly perform with theater productions, both in the schools and out in our community."

"That sounds wonderful, and I still want to sing, a cappella, and I know Hillyer has a group that does that."

"Right, you'll be busy."

℘

That night Cassie fell into a troubled sleep. She awoke in a sweat after something in her dream screamed. Her trembling stopped after she took deep breaths.

"Dear God, it all felt so real," she shook her head.

She turned on her bedside lamp and grabbed her bible. She read the 23rd Psalm, words that always calmed her.

"Admit it, Cassie," she whispered, "you're super sensitive, always have been, mom's death, dad's leaving to rejoin his Green Beret group, it's all part of living. I gotta just trust, and move through all this. It's gonna be an exciting year. Let this bad cruddy stuff go."

She turned off her light. A night bird singing out in the backyard helped put her back to sleep.

℘

Maggie listened as her granddaughter and the Hillyer counselor went over Cassie's schedule.

"I believe you'll do just fine, with your time-management ability, your grades from Smith High School, outstanding. What do you think, Cassie?"

"I'll give it all my best effort. Hillyer Academy classes will be super harder than anything I've experienced. I'm a little concerned about calculus. And I appreciate your advice about getting signed up for the PSAT in October. That test will be a good gauge of how well I really'm doing."

Cassie watched Mrs. Brooks smile to her, "You sound very serious about your studies. You're exactly the kind of student we work with best, so we can send you on to a fine university in three years."

"I'm excited about AP Chemistry. I already think I know where I'm headed, to microbiology as my college major, and I've a couple of different schools in mind."

"We'll be helping you every step of the way. I'll be your counselor through your next three years. That's how we do it at Hillyer. Each counselor advises an entire class that we see through to students' graduations. We really get to know our students by the end of that time."

"Great, and thanks, ma'am," Cassie rose and shook hands with her counselor.

Maggie raised her hand and nodded to the counselor from her seat in the back of the counselor's office.

They walked out of the stately red brick building and down the steps to the visitor parking area.

"Grandma, I'm getting really excited for classes to start next week. Did you listen when Mrs. Brooks told me how much longer the school year is at Hillyer?"

"I did; this school tries very hard to prep you for university work."

"It'll be intense."

Maggie put her arm around her granddaughter's shoulder, "I have every confidence in you, my dear."

2

Cassie ran up the steps to the library five minutes after it opened on Thursday morning. She pulled her backpack off at a reference table and took out her photos.

"The banner pictures turned out, oh, nice. Wish me luck, granddad," Cassie looked up, imaging her granddad smiling to her. She headed to the checkout desk. There was no one behind her so she made her initial request for help.

"Young lady, we've got a staff member who'll be able to point you in the right direction."

She directed Cassie to an office in the back part of the library. Cassie looked around at the bright, cheerful facility as she walked past rows and rows of books. She stopped at a stack near the back office. She took in a deep breath.

"My favorite is the smell of you guys, you books, some old and funny smelling, but lots are newer."

She touched several books, remembering all her years of going to the libraries on and off the bases where the Montclare's lived. The door was open, but she knocked. After introducing herself, Cassie plunged in with her research question, bringing out the pictures of the banner.

"My goodness, your granddad and dad gave you quite a task."

"What do ya think?"

"Come with me."

She walked behind Mrs. Reinhold as they progressed through a musty row of books.

"I'd use these two to start with. I wish I could let you check them out, but I can't, since they're reference. But you're welcome to visit us as much as you can, to look through the information. Here, one for you, and I'll carry this one."

She handed Cassie the heavier of the two reference books.

Cassie sat at a table near a window out to the bright sunshine. She watched the trees waving in the wind.

"Girl, you're going to be doing some letter writing," she determined after she looked at the list of college and universities with sports teams, back in the 1920's.

She remembered telling Mrs. Reinhold where her granddad attended the university and veterinary school. The librarian agreed with Cassie about researching schools in Georgia and Alabama. She started to go through the information about schools in those two states in the 1920's.

After 15 minutes Mrs. Reinhold came back to her. She suggested a third book which she brought with her. Cassie looked at the beginning table of contents.

"Thanks Mrs. Reinhold, I told you the banner probably belonged to a sports team. So the history of athletics at schools will be important."

"You remember where these books are kept?"

"Right, I'll just head to them the next time I'm here, really appreciate your help."

"You'll let me know how your adventure goes; I'm anxious to hear where this banner belongs."

"I'll keep you up to date, so sweet, you helping me, thanks Mrs. Reinhold."

∿∿

By Friday of her first week in Ephrine Cassie began to feel comfortable staying in her grandma's home. She realized it was her own now. She could look ahead to the prospect of the school year in a new school. As the clinic quieted down that Friday afternoon, Maggie gave Cassie money so she could walk to the transportation center several blocks away. She needed to pay for two months of bus passes. Cassie would ride the city bus to and from Hillyer Academy.

"You and I talked about this, Cassie. I sometimes have early surgery, so you must have reliable transportation."

She stood with her grandma in her office.

"I completely understand, GMag. I'm glad to be on my own, getting to and from school, after all the years of nannies, mom and dad taking me when they could. It sure makes me feel more responsible for myself."

"Good, dear heart, now scoot," Maggie paused, "you're getting so grownup."

Cassie hustled out of the clinic and walked fast to the transportation center. Earlier in the week she did a practice ride on the bus to and from Hillyer to see how it would work out. This gave her a good gauge for how long it would take her to walk to the transport center from her home, and from the transport center to Hillyer Academy. It turned out to be 15 and 15, 15 minutes to walk, and 15 minutes to ride with the stops included.

As the transport center cashier gave her a receipt and bus tickets, she told Cassie there were lots of Humphrey University students riding the bus.

Cassie decided not to mention to her that she was in high school.

"Do I look like a college student?" she asked herself as she headed back to the clinic. Then she remembered that Hillyer Academy and Humphrey University actually bordered each other. She shook her head, knowing she would always be identified by her bright Hillyer uniform.

∽

"I'm excited to start dance again, GMag."

"I want you to have fun, plus expand your dance knowledge and experience. Let's get your bike out. I've decided you can ride your bike home from dance class."

"Have to, Grandma, Saturdays can be busy at the clinic. You're needed there for the animals."

"Thanks for understanding."

Maggie walked in with Cassie after she locked up her bike at the rack in front of the Recreation Center. Cassie looked at the group of dancers as she entered the large room where they would always meet.

"Wow, two faces I recognize, Emma, and Annie. That's so good, I'll know somebody. They were nice girls last summer," Cassie thought as she moved into the room.

"Thank you, Grandma, for all this. It sure will add to my year, more expertise in dance."

They hugged.

"Have a good day, Grandma."

Maggie nodded to Cassie, "Have fun."

Cassie sat on the floor in the second row of the group.

"Thanks for getting in place so quickly. I can tell we're gonna get along great."

The group giggled to their teacher who introduced herself as Laura. She spoke for a couple minutes about her own dance background. Then she called roll, asking each girl to give her a preferred nickname.

"Cass Margaret Montclare."

"Here," she raised her hand, "Please call me Cassie."

Laura nodded her head to Cassie and smiled to her, "Got it."

Half way through the class the girls got a five minute water break.

Emma and Annie sat with Cassie.

"We're glad you're back, and we're hoping you're doing OK, last summer so tough for you."

"Thanks, Emma."

She smiled to the teens and nodded.

"I'm glad, so happy I get to spend the whole school year dancing in classes. Last summer I was just here in August."

"You're here for school?"

"Gosh, you couldn't know, Annie. I'm living with my grandma, Maggie Montclare, be staying with her until I go on to university."

"Can we ask, is," Emma paused as Cassie watched her forehead furrow, "is your dad OK?"

"Oh yeah, he's rejoining his Green Beret unit. When my mom died, the Army changed his duty assignment at Fort Bragg. But that year is up, so back he goes to his special ops assignment."

"Will you get to see him, Cassie?"

"Probably not for a while, he'll be all over the world. He wanted me in a stable situation, which my grandma is in."

"She's our dog's vet," Annie nodded.

"Ours too," agreed Emma.

The class switched from ballet to modern dance half way through. After that hour Cassie felt pulls and aches in lots of muscles in her arms, back and legs. The three girls gathered their belongings as a tall young man with dark blonde hair walked up to them.

"How's class, Sis?"

"Tiring," Annie sighed, "uh, Cassie, this is my brother, Luke."

Cassie shook his hand and looked up into his bright brown eyes.

"Hi Luke."

He smiled to her and swallowed hard, after taking in her lithe body, her shape accentuated by the black leotard and tights.

"Hi Cassie, uh, I'm dropping Emma off before we go home. Wanna ride?"

"I have my bike, but I'm exhausted, no real exercising for a few days. Do you have room for my bike in your trunk?"

"Course."

Luke took Emma home first. He helped Cassie unload her bike and walked it up to the front porch steps.

"Thanks, I'll take it from here. I sure appreciate the ride," she looked into his chocolate eyes as she gave him her wide smile.

He couldn't take his eyes off her.

"Where'll you be at school?"

"Sophomore at Hillyer."

Instant disappointment hit him square in his stomach. He thought, "There'll be no chance to meet her in a school setting."

He paused, "Well, see ya, Cassie."

He smiled, his eye contact intense on her eyes.

"Uh huh, see ya."

Back in the car he drove to their home.

"Cassie was in our dance class last August. She'd come here to be with her grandma, that's Dr. Montclare, our vet. Cassie's mom just died. She was so sad, but dance class helped perk her up."

"She is one outanding-looking young lady."

"I agree, but she's not aware of how beautiful she is. She was one sad and confused kid while she was here."

"You'll be going to Hillyer, Annie, so you'll get to see her, kinda keep track of how she's doing, right?"

"Uh huh, I will, she, Emma and me, we already had the beginning of a friendship going with her a year ago. It'll be fun to get to know her better, 'specially since Emma will be at Ephrine High."

"I agree, that will be so good for you."

He looked over to his sister. He remembered that last year was her strongest year, since she'd gotten sick.

"I'll keep watching over Annie, like I've always done, Mom and Dad, they gotta work, the unbelievable expenses. But I'm glad she's at Hillyer; she's super smart. I belong at Ephrine High, but Annie doesn't," Luke thought.

"So Cassie, tell me about her."

"Army brat, dad's a Green Beret, living with Dr. Montclare, dad's assigned all over the world, wherever there's unrest."

"Stability, that's what she needs."

"Right, hey, you're asking lots of questions, are you interested in her?"

"Am, but she's a sophomore, like you guys, maybe not dating."

"Pretty much the way it is."

Luke parked his sedan on the concrete slab to the left of the two car garage. They went in together.

"Bro, I'm gonna lie down. Mom and Dad should be back from the wedding in a little while."

"Yeah, go rest. I'm gonna do a run. Actual cross country practice starts next week, a week and a half before classes begin."

Luke changed into his running shorts and t-shirt and headed out.

"My own neighborhood's a great place to run; we got hills, and more hills," he spoke out as he headed up the fifth hill in his surrounding area.

In his junior year Luke would run cross country in the fall and play soccer in the spring. He helped at home with the cooking Mondays through Thursdays. He also cleaned house, doing two bathrooms and vacuuming the house, including his own bedroom. His parents kept up their bedroom and master bath. His mom handled the wash and grocery shopping, and his dad did the yardwork. Annie cleaned her own bedroom and watched over Pep, the family dog. She took him for walks, fed him, and cleaned up after him out in the back yard.

Luke decided he never wanted to be a CPA, his dad was that; tax season had hideous elements. His lawyer mom worked for a firm that handled lots of family issues. From the stories she told, he decided lawyering wasn't for him either.

Like Saint Luke of ancient times, Luke planned on being a doctor. He had his sights set on a university degree, taking his MCAT's and on to medical school. Even as a little boy he helped with sick folks or sick pets. After his sister got better from being so ill, that sealed the deal. One day he would be Dr. Ingraham.

"I have so much hope for modern medical technology, it's getting better and better all the time," he would tell his friends. "I've seen that in how well my sister is doing."

He finished his run and washed up at the kitchen sink. All he heard was the AC air moving through his home. He checked on Annie. She lay on her bed with her body turned toward the door. He stepped in to check on her breathing. Then he noticed. Little light purple circles formed right under her eyes.

He moved out of her room and sat on the first step of the stairway down to the first floor. He put his arms on his knees and held his head in his hands. His throat engorged to the point of choking him, and his stomach started flipping around.

"God, help our family, help Annie," he whispered as tears burned his eyes.

ℂ

"Father, thank you for seeing us on a Sunday afternoon."

"Of course, tell me about how everything's going for you two."

He looked at Maggie.

"Yes, I still have my sad times, but I'm coping much better. Cassie, just by her presence in my home, is such a comfort to me."

Maggie touched her granddaughter's shoulder, and they nodded to each other.

"The clinic's motoring along, like a well-oiled machine. Our new vet, Brad, is working out so well. Matter of fact, he's taking on many calls outside the community, on families' farms and ranches. That's something I could not handle. That relieves me to carry on the practice, do the surgeries that we can in our clinic setting. Big stuff, as always, I make sure the animals get transported to the UGA Vet School, if that's possible."

"And you Cassie, let's see, it's near the end of September, so you have some weeks of school under your belt. What do you think?"

"Father, Hillyer Academy, it's rigorous."

"So I've heard."

"Usually four hours of homework a night, AP Chem and the a cappella part of my chorus class, those are my favorites. Actually, I like the discipline, the uniforms, it's what I grew up with," she paused and smiled to Father, "Army strong."

"That's good."

"God's with me, always. Oh, and dad called last night. He can't tell us where he is, only that he's AOK. He sounded pleased with my report of how school's going. And I told him about my two friends, and about a boy I'm starting to like a lot."

Father offered several suggestions about coping with the sadness they both still felt. They held hands around the small round table as Father said a prayer with them.

℘

"Anything special you want to do for your birthday, Cassie?"

"Just go out to dinner with you, Grandma, I know dad will try to call. I want a quiet time, like last year, 'cept then I just had dad. And well, friends, I'm still getting to know people, so not gonna mention about a birthday. Truth, sometime this weekend, I'd just like to climb that big hill outside of town. It's a popular trail."

"That's it?"

"Yeah, I'm realizing how important regular exercising is. I sit so much studying and being in class."

"Right, I don't sit much at all, and I feel good because of the standing and moving with my big and little patients."

"So as often as I can, I'll get up and do a run early in the morning, just around in the neighborhood."

"Sounds like a plan. And Cassie, I'd love to hike up the hill with you, Sunday afternoon?"

"Great."

೮ා

At lunch in early October Annie mentioned to Cassie about CYO at St Luke's.

"Luke and I go to CYO (Catholic Youth Organization); it's at 10:30, then we attend mass at 11:30. Wanta get involved? Luke drives me. He says he could pick you up the three Sundays a month that we meet."

"Gosh, that's a group I'd like to be with, I think."

"That's why I asked; it sounded like you guys did a couple of community projects back at Bragg."

"Yeah we did, at my old church, to give back. At our age it's hard to think about giving back to the community."

"Yeah, we're super intensely focused on just ourselves."

Annie and Cassie looked at each other. They nodded

"I'll check with my grandma. We always go to early mass so we have the rest of the day free. I'd need to get up early and catch up on homework."

"Let me know."

"Thanks, Annie."

೮ා

The teens gathered their backpacks with their dance gear inside. Luke stopped by to take Annie, Emma and Cassie home from class.

"Luke, I got ready real quick, I wanted to talk to you, just you and me. Can we go outside and find a private place for a minute before they come out?"

They stood facing each other under the shade of a tree near the rec center entrance.

Cassie looked up into his eyes, "Somethin's not right with Annie. Today she left the group twice during practice to sit down and have water. I've noticed her energy level at school is down. But the worst thing is her beautiful eyes; they've lost that shine she had when she smiles."

Annie watched tears glint Luke's eyes.

"Sorry, you need to know, Annie's been in remission, ALL."

He shook his head, "Acute lymphoblastic leukemia."

"Oh," she paused, "my," another pause, "gosh."

She kept shaking her head.

"No one's said a word to me about her being ill."

"Five years, remission, but I noticed her eyes, in August, when I first met you. I knew then, that, the cancer, well, it is no longer in remission."

"My mom died of a brain tumor. It went fast for her. Is Annie going to be able to finish up the semester?"

"Course, she's fighting this thing every step of the way. She wants to continue to dance, and be with you and Emma, wants her life to go on, just as it's been. She faces each day with a fortitude that I'm so proud of."

"Luke, there must be so many things that she wants to do while she still can."

Cassie looked up into his eyes.

"Uh, not really, she enjoys each day, doesn't think much about tomorrow."

"Gosh, I get so fearful sometimes, I gotta learn to be just in this day only, like the way Annie does. How's she do it?" she pleaded with him.

Cassie started to shake and cry, cries turning into sobs. Luke took her in his arms and held her in a close hug.

"God's with Annie, every step of her way, just like God's with you and me. Don't be afraid."

He let go of her. She stepped back and wiped her tears away with her hands. They stood, looking at each other.

"That comforted me, what you just said. You're gonna be a great doctor, one day," she nodded.

Luke's eyes widened as she made her comment.

"How could she know?" he wondered. He thought about it for a moment, "her intuition, yeah, even at her age."

Emma and Annie came into their sight.

She looked up to him again, "Thanks for telling me; I'll let Annie fill me in when she's ready."

"Good."

"Me and Annie," Emma paused, "we just been talking, Halloween's coming up."

"What you guys wanna do?" Luke questioned them as he drove toward Emma's home.

"Luke, I want to go trick or treating, yeah, I'm a little old, but I'd like to go."

"Us girls, we'll dress up and visit a few homes in Annie's neighborhood."

"I've got an old days costume I could wear," Cassie spoke up.

"Me, too."

"I think my witch costume from a few years back will still work for me. It's in the back of my closet with a witch's hat to go with the black outfit," Annie breathed out. "It'll be fun; we'll come back to our house. My folks sit with us and we all help with the reading of scary stories after trick or treating. It's a special Halloween tradition."

"Let's do it."

They high-fived each other as they sat in the back seat.

Once they left Emma's home, Cassie shared about CYO.

"Grandma thinks it's great for me to be with the group. And she really appreciates that you'll pick me up and bring me home after church the three weeks a month the group meets. That's a big chaperone job you have Luke.

Are you OK with that?"

He turned and flashed a smile to Annie and her.

"Course, I'm going, Annie's going, we're happy to pick you up and take you home."

ℬ

Cassie sat by herself in the lunchroom. Annie went home, not feeling well, after second period. She opened up her sack lunch.

"My favorites, pb&j, apple cut up, two chocolate chip bars which I made myself."

She opened her carton of chocolate milk and took a sip. She looked up to see a tall, large-framed guy walk over to her.

"Oh crap," she whispered.

"Mind if I sit down, I see your friend isn't here."

"Yeah, Annie got sick in second period, had to go home."

Cassie continued to look up at him and finally gave him eye contact. Then she nodded her head.

He sat down and extended his hand, "I'm Ian, and I am so sorry for my words to you when you helped me with Dover. My mouth always has and continues to get me in trouble."

He shook his head, his lips set in a thin line.

"OK, what does he want?" Cassie asked herself as she accepted his hand. They shook twice and let go.

"You're new to Hillyer; where'd you go to school last year?"

Cassie went on to tell him a quick version of her year before Hillyer.

"So sorry about your mom. I lost my grandpap last year. There'll be lots more folks that we'll lose in the next years."

Cassie nodded to him. They sat, eating their lunches. Cassie said nothing, but she felt a kind of quiet peace, a comfort by the fact that he sat there, across from her. They began to finish up their food.

"I've an extra chocolate chip bar, want it?"

"Yeah, I love those things."

"Made the batch myself; I do most of the desserts at grandma's. She's too busy with her practice to do baking."

He finished off the bar in three bites.

"Outstanding, so tasty, thanks."

Cassie stood up and gathered her trash, leaving her place at the table clean.

"See ya," she spoke in a quiet tone as she nodded to him.

Cassie dumped her trash and headed for the library until her next class.

"Wonder how he's getting along in our AP chem class, about died when I saw him that first day of class," she remembered the huge lump in her throat as class started that first day. Within several minutes she forgot him as her instructor launched them into the world of chemistry.

⅀

A hushed silence surrounded the teens and parents before Chuck Ingraham began the final story. They heard only the hissing and cracking of logs burning in the fireplace. Chuck's deep voice resonated throughout the darkened living room. Annie held one of Cassie hands and Emma held the other. Annie started to shiver which caught on with the other two. When he shouted BOO, the girls screamed. He proceeded on as soon as they stopped the noise.

"Awesome, those super scary stories, will I be able to sleep tonight?" Emma asked.

The girls laughed with her.

"Uh, nuthin' keeps you from sleep, you old sleepy head," Annie spoke up.

"Right."

"Well, I don't know about you guys, but I'm keeping my bed stand light on, just for comfort," Cassie chimed in.

"Grandma'll be here in a minute, what a blast that storytelling was, I gotta remember, scary stories from places in Pennsylvania, thanks you guys."

Emma and Cassie told parts of two scary stories they remembered to Maggie as she drove Emma home.

As they pulled into the garage, Cassie asked, "Did you have many trick- or-treaters?"

"A few, there are several young families who've moved in and renovated their homes in our area. The little kids' outfits, delightful."

"GMag, I hadn't been trick or treating for four years, a Halloween party one year. But the neatest, wow, the scary stories."

"Pretty scared?"

"I was. And the atmosphere in the Ingraham living room, the fire in the fireplace, the lights turned way down, and Annie's dad, he has this super cool, very low voice, a bass voice."

"Grandma, can we talk?"

They sat at the breakfast nook. Cassie laid out the candy she picked up while on their outing.

Maggie waited for her granddaughter.

"Help yourself, GMag."

"Uuummm, chocolate with nuts, my favorite, and it's just a little candy bar. That's good. You know what a sweet tooth I've got."

"Just like mine," Cassie smiled to her grandma.

"Annie's bad sick."

"Tell me."

"Been in remission from ALL for five years, but it's back. She's sayin' nuthin' but her brother, Luke, and I talked."

"It's back, really?"

Cassie nodded, "Remember how I watched mom get sick and die right in front of my eyes, in just a few weeks. Well, I'm seeing that in Annie. She's limping and gets bruised way too easy. Plus her energy level is way down, says she's barely getting her homework done every night. You know how much we have."

"Yeah, that's for sure."

Maggie remembered the four hours Cassie spent on homework every night, and weekend mornings and afternoons.

"Is what I'm having you do around our home too much for you?"

"No way, I got a high energy level. As you've seen, the chores get done. Grandma, what can I do?"

"Be her friend, Cassie, in the time she's got left, before she gets so weak all she'll be able to do is smile as you hold her hand."

"One more thing, Grandma."

Maggie nodded to her.

"The last time Annie missed school a boy came to me inquiring about her and about her missing school. The boy told me he really liked her; they have a class together. He's in my AP Chem class. I don't know how to handle this, except maybe have him join us for lunch. We just get 30 minutes, enough time to buy our milk and eat our lunches from home."

"That sounds good, Cassie. You're old enough to play matchmaker."

"But you gotta know, it's that guy who made that sexual comment to me while I was helping you this summer."

"Ian Sjarlendone?"

"Yeah, the preacher's kid."

"He's a student at Hillyer?"

"Uh huh, running cross country now, same as Luke, Annie's brother. But Luke's at Ephrine High."

"You never told me."

"Didn't want to, but he seems interested in Annie. I think he needs to know the truth about her."

Maggie put her hand over Cassie's.

"You must let her tell him, in her own way."

"Whew, glad you suggested that, 'cause it's none of my business."

"That's right, health stuff, that's a big deal privacy issue."

"For sure, people didn't know what was really going on with mom until near the end. We kept hoping for a miracle."

Cassie burst into tears. Maggie held on to her hand with a stronger hold.

She let Cassie cry and handed her a tissue when she calmed down. Cassie looked into her grandma's blue eyes, took several deep breaths and shook her head.

"The miracle became God taking mom to heaven, no more suffering. That's the miracle for Annie, I know it," she whispered.

ℂ

And so that's how Ian and Annie met. He joined them at lunch on Monday of the next week. And, with Cassie there, he said he wanted to get to know her.

"Well, you need to know, I hope to see this Christmas."

Cassie watched Ian's forehead crease and his face blanch white. Annie explained to him about her condition and how she planned to stay at Hillyer for as long as she could, to learn as much as she could.

As Annie went on talking to them, a parallel thought raced through Cassie's mind.

"I didn't realize how quick this leukemia takes over. I pray Annie will see Christ's birth," she thought and then returned to Annie's conversation.

"My dear God, I feel so helpless," Ian shook his head to them and looked into Annie's eyes. "You don't look sick, Annie."

"I know, it's inside me. Cassie knows, been watching me, my dancing days at dance class are almost over. I'm getting weaker every day; it's moving way beyond medicine's ability to control."

"Special things you want to do?"

"Just live each day as fully as I can. Remember, we're not in charge."

Cassie spoke up, "But God is."

"I can be your friend, Annie."

She looked over to him, "Yeah, you can be."

They finished their lunches and headed out to their next classes.

Cassie resolved before she stepped into the classroom, "Be a friend, me too, I will continue to be a friend."

₧

Charley smiled to them, "Wow, everybody came. I know Luke's in a cross-country meet, so he's excused. Inside paint team, you guys, are you ready?"

"We are."

The two painters walked into the Oarcini home. The couple had the living room furniture pulled out into the middle so the paint team had enough room to work. With the curtains removed from around the window, the two proceeded, one teen painting from the bottom up ahead of the teen painting from the top down on each wall. Once they finished they would paint a second coat, to completely cover the old wall color. Within 10 minutes the two of them saw the room begin to brighten up, from the old drabness.

A second team worked outside on ladders repainting the house trim all around the small one story home.

"Lookin' good," Charley, team leader, cheered as he watched their progress.

Cassie kept going up and down, moving the ladder as she repainted the trim on one side of the house. In several places she used a putty knife to remove peeling paint.

Two teams worked on the leaf raking. Annie helped with that effort, bagging up leaves into the large paper sacks that the city wanted folks to use. After the backyard got cleared of leaves, a teen used the family lawn mower to cut the straggly grass that lay beneath the leaves. Finally a teen set up the sprinkler and watered the very dry grass.

Once an area in the front yard got cleared of leaves, the group stopped to have the sandwiches one of the parents prepared. Another parent brought cookies, fruit, and sodas. Everyone stopped inside the front door to see the progress of the painters. They were almost finished.

"Hey, the room looks awesome, think the family will be pleased?"

Cassie and Annie heard claps and cheers all around. The house trim turned out good, and applause went round for that effort after they all had a chance to see the painters' work.

Everyone wanted to finish by 2 p.m. so the front yard effort went into high gear. Leaves cleared, lawn mowed and watered, that was the goal. Several teens helped inside, clearing the ladder used for the high painting. One person pulled the blue tape away from the baseboard and another one removed the paint that oozed a couple of places onto the baseboard. Then he pulled up the papers used to protect the floor.

Parents gathered with the CYO members, to pick the kids up, and to take the stepladders. Father Paul appeared and saw the efforts. He counted 22 bags of leaves that Ephrine Sanitation would pick up on Monday. Everyone gathered around him. His eyes went around the group, making sure he made eye contact with each teen.

He nodded his head and smiled to them, "I'm very proud of you all. This family really needed our help, and they got it. The Oarcini's are in the eighties, still wanting to be together in their own home. I know they're grateful, and you'll hear from them."

Annie's mom took Cassie home, and then headed home with her daughter.

"I'll take a shower and lie down. It was so much fun to help out, to see the little miracle we performed for that church family."

Jennifer stood looking at her dirty and tired daughter. She came to her with a gentle hug.

"Awesome effort, Annie, I'm very proud of you pitching in."

"I wanted to, Mom, I felt really strong until the last hour."

It was quiet in the Ingraham home. Annie's mom went about her Saturday chores. She looked in on Annie and found her sleeping, lying down on her side.

"My beautiful, wonderful daughter, she wants to help, for as long as she can."

Jennifer left her daughter's side and partially closed the bedroom door. Like a knife easing into her heart, Jennifer felt a horrific pain surging through her entire body.

"Loss, it's happening to me, to Luke, to Annie's dad," she held her head, as she slid down the wall in the hall away from her daughter's bedroom.

She put her head on her knees and felt hot tears dropping on her legs. She prayed, five Our Father's and five Hail Mary's. She felt better and started in on what was next on her list of Saturday chores.

"Thank you God, for the power of prayer," she whispered.

She squared her shoulders and started to smile.

"Luke'll be home soon, hope his cross country meet went well."

ⅎ

"Where's Annie?" Cassie asked as Luke picked her up for CYO before church that Sunday.

Luke turned to look at Cassie. She watched tears glaze his eyes. He shook his head.

"I expected this, Luke. She did way too much yesterday, but she loved being with our group."

"None of us realize how fast and how sick she's gotten. I hope she celebrates Christmas with us."

"Me too."

"Cassie, Annie's told me about your special project you're doing for your dad and your granddad. I like doing research, finding answers to, well, especially like the HIV, stuff like that. I do reading on that topic. Would you like some help?

"Really, help me?"

They walked from the parking lot to the church.

"Honest truth, Cassie, I want to spend time with you."

She stopped and touched his shoulder. She lifted her head and looked into his eyes.

"I want to spend time with you, Luke. The banner project, yeah, I'm deep into it. And I need help."

"Good, we'll figure it out."

Before they walked into the meeting room, she whispered to him.

"Time, spend time with your sister, while you can. I plan to visit her."

"Hey, we can work on the project at our place; that way you can see Annie too."

Cassie smiled to him and nodded.

ℍ

"Dad, how are you?"

Cassie's dad gave her several sentences of information about himself.

"Can't say anymore, Cassie, but know that I think of you every single day. I just had to call you. The picture you sent of your group in front of the house you helped fix up, it was a super effort. I'm proud of you for volunteering for your community and for the family in your home church."

"Do you ever get to church?"

"Not often, but I say prayers, have a prayer list, with you and grandma at the top of the list."

"Dad."

"Tell me."

"I have a boy I really like, Luke. His sister, Annie, is my friend. She's dying, Dad."

"Cancer?"

"Yeah, leukemia, she's been in remission, but this is the end.

Cassie paused, "Dad."

"Tell me."

"Luke's helping me with the banner. I take my project to the Ingraham home; Annie offers suggestions too."

"Good, I love you, Cassie. I got just another minute. Can I talk to grandma?"

"Love you, Dad, be safe."

Cassie handed the phone over to Maggie.

ℴ

She heard her grandma working in the kitchen as she peeked out the window to view the clear Georgia sky.

"Thanksgiving, yay, it's Thanksgiving, a happy time for grandma and me," Cassie sang out as she dressed in preparation for the noon potluck.

Every year Maggie invited her entire medical team to her home for a celebration of the holiday. Kay Ann and Analease brought their husbands and children. Miriam always came alone; she remained single and liked it that way. The new vet partner, Brad, came with his girlfriend. Cassie marveled at how organized the team was, each family bringing food for the gathering. All Maggie had to do was warm up the ham and provide the cups, paper plates, napkins and plastic cutlery. The group handled the rest of the potluck.

Cassie went to her grandma, "GMag, this kinda looks like getting set up for a surgery."

Maggie gave Cassie a hug, "It's a well-oiled machine, just like at the office."

They ate around both the kitchen and dining room tables. Folks also sat on folding chairs and balanced their food on their knees, their drinks on the floor near them.

"Delicious, you all can cook," Brad spoke out after folks began finishing up their first plates of food.

"Yeah, Brad, this is your first year with this food-loving crew, wait 'til you get to dessert, you better save room," Analease warned him.

The conversation, always, surrounded football, how the university teams were holding up, UGA, and Georgia Tech, and then the lower division football teams. Talk moved to the local football teams, Ephrine High, and Hillyer Academy. And finally, since there were so many different pro teams represented in the group, there was discussion of the respective teams, and the chances of which team was Super Bowl bound.

"Five, count 'em, wow, five desserts," Cassie announced as she set the pies, cakes, and cheese cake out on the kitchen counter.

"Best part of the meal, the desserts," Maggie called out.

Cheers and applause followed her comment.

"One bite, oh my, this pumpkin pie, my favorite," Brad declared.

"That's because you piled yummy whipped cream on top," Maggie looked over and observed his plate of dessert.

"No, I declare the chocolate cake with chocolate frosting, that's the best," Analease's husband spoke up.

"I'm gonna try small servings of several different desserts," Cassie said to the little boy sitting next to her.

He looked up to her and smiled.

The guests left about 2:30 after everyone helped with cleanup.

"GMag, awesome to use disposable dish, glass, and silverware. We just had the pan for ham to clean up."

"Right, all my medical crew have to work tomorrow. It'll be a busy Friday."

"If it's OK, I'll ride my bike to the Ingraham home tomorrow; we're working on the banner project. Annie's enjoying helping us too."

"Perfectly fine, hope you can take some time for yourself, Cassie, before Monday. Remember, we have plans for Saturday afternoon."

"I will take time, but I'm psyched about granddad's project."

3

"I've checked three times, using the big book of colleges and universities, against the addresses on your list."

"Thanks, Annie, now it's up to Cassie and me to get these letters written."

The teens asked and got help from Annie and Luke's mom and from Maggie about the letter to send.

"Should it be word processed or hand written?"

With the adults' input Cassie decided that a letter neatly written on nice stationery along with a picture of the banner was the way to approach the letters.

"It's more personalized, and the reader will know it's a young person writing," Cassie nodded to Luke and Annie.

"Time for me to go rest, you two carry on."

Cassie gazed at Annie, "Don't tear up, you dope," she told herself.

"Thanks for your help," she smiled to Annie.

For the next two hours Luke and Cassie sat across from each other at the dining room table, writing letters and addressing envelopes to colleges inquiring about the banner. They each copied from a sample letter Cassie printed out in big letters. Luke's mom edited the inquiry letter to make sure it asked for the information Cassie needed to match the banner with the school.

"Wow, 11 done, that's super neat, Luke. I'll finish up the last one at home and get them ready for mailing."

"You'll make sure you do some kind of spreadsheet, you know, listing all your addresses, the date sent, so you can keep track, if you hear from the schools."

"Got it, Luke, thanks for helping me with the organization of the project. I really had no idea," she stopped short.

"Yeah, it's a big deal, finding out where the banner belongs, your grandpa's wish. I want you to keep me filled in as you get answers back. I think sending the letter to the college's research librarian's a good plan."

"Hope so, I know the lady at our city library sure's been a help to me."

Luke walked her out to her bike parked in front of his car.

"That big plastic folder's great for keeping all your project."

"Yeah, GMag said the same thing, stuff wouldn't get wet. And the backpack protects too."

"I like being with you, Cassie. I want to keep seeing you."

Cassie lifted up her arms and came into a hug with him.

She whispered, "Want ta see you, we'll still have CYO, but not this Sunday 'cause of Thanksgiving."

They let go of each other and Luke shook his head.

"Think next week will be Annie's last actually attending Hillyer. My folks've hired a Hillyer teacher to come to our home to help Annie with her school work in the afternoons for as long as she's able."

"Good."

"Know one of her goals is to complete this semester and enjoy Christmas."

"Before I go, I gotta ask, are you and your folks getting help with what's happening, with Annie?"

Cassie heard him exhale a big breath. She watched his slow nod to her.

"Hospice, they're the pros, nuthin' can really get us ready, but we're working with them."

"Uh huh, that's what happened for dad and me with mom. She wanted to be home so bad at the end. But she got so incredibly sick; her end came in the hospital."

"Cassie, don't know how you did it."

She touched his upper arm.

"One day at a time," she nodded as he watched tears stud her eyes.

"See ya."

"See ya."

She looked back as she pedaled away from his home. He waved, and she waved back.

&

"Last stop, Cassie, we've completed our Christmas shopping, as I always do, directly after Thanksgiving. I'm glad we waited until this Saturday afternoon. Yesterday the mobs came out."

"For sure, Grandma, uh," Cassie paused, "why we goin' into this shop?"

"You've told me you want to attend Hillyer's Holiday Ball. I checked your closet. You need a dress."

Cassie watched her grandma's big smile to her.

"Oh my gosh, I really don't have anything for a fancy dance like that."

"Exactly why we're here, my dear."

Cassie looked through the selection of dresses and picked three. She modeled for her grandma.

"You go for the simple, classic look, Cassie."

"Uh huh, and I gotta think about that I'll have two more Holiday Balls after this year. So I'll wear the dress several times. I just don't like clothes much; that's why being in uniform is so great for me."

"I can't decide," as Cassie held all three dresses for her grandma to look over. "You'll have to pick."

"Not fair, Cassie."

"Uh huh, it's fair, you have good taste. Your clothes out of the clinic, so nice, you keep your young look."

"Magenta, or light blue, or the pale pink, hhhmmm," Maggie mused. "The pale pink, brings out your bright blue eyes, yes, that's the dress."

They found shoes with tiny heels to go with the dress, from the same shop.

"I'm tired, it's been a long day, but tomorrow we can relax. Shopping's done, and we'll go to early mass, then the rest of the day is our own. Right, you don't have your group?"

"Not until next Sunday."

"Pizza night, what cha think?"

"Yeah, I'm so hungry, Grandma."

As they sat having pizza at the dining room table, Cassie smiled as she thought about her Christmas present for her grandma.

"I'm so glad I've spent time at the clinic. GMag needs a spare stethoscope to work with her animals. Kay Ann mentioned she had a hard time keeping track of the good one she has. So Kay Ann's ordering it for me. And dad's sent me the money to buy it."

"You've been somewhere else," Maggie shook her head to her granddaughter.

"Christmas thoughts," she nodded as she brought out the pieces of apple pie she saved back for them from the Thanksgiving meal.

ℂ

"How'd it go?" Luke asked as he picked up Cassie for CYO several weeks later.

"Second place, oh Luke, the dancers, so much talent, in all the different dance schools. It'll be a great gauge, for our group to go beyond the abilities of some of the most talented girls."

"Do you want to do other stuff with dance besides competition?"

"Yeah, we have theater productions here in Ephrine, and at Hillyer. I want to get involved with them. But I gotta show grandma I can handle the schoolwork first. So that's my goal starting next summer, to expand out and dance other places."

They held hands as they walked to the room where CYO met before church.

"Luke."

"What, Cassie?"

"I really want to go to Hillyer's Holiday Ball. Would you come with me as my date?"

He stopped, let go of her hand and turned to her. He agreed, provided it was a date and time that would work for his family.

"Annie's declining so fast. I'll let you know, and thanks for asking me."

She finally saw him smile.

All through CYO Cassie felt a guilty pang swirling around her.

"I'm having fun, planning to go to a ball, and Annie's dying. God, you're sure this is what you want for me?"

But she didn't get an answer from God. She rode her bike to Annie's several times after she got home from school those final weeks of the semester. They talked about the dance competition and about the upcoming Hillyer Holiday Music Fest. Annie told her about her good grades in all her classes.

"Did you get your dress for the dance?"

"I did."

"It's?"

"Pale pink, swirly skirt, ¾ length sleeves, small collar."

"Classic."

"It's gotta be for another year or two."

"Right, I'm having my own ball here in our living room."

Cassie noticed Annie's small smile.

"Ian's coming over, dressin' up, to dance with me. We've picked out a CD to dance to."

"Slow music?"

"Yeah, Christmasy, but still kinda romantic music. I'm hoping to still be able to stand up and dance."

"Good Annie, I'm so happy that you'll have your ball, just like I will at Hillyer."

"Cassie."

"Yeah?"

"Luke's very excited to be going to the dance with you. You're the first girl who's ever asked him to do stuff."

"Really?"

"Yeah, he's a pretty shy dude, too wrapped up with me; promise you'll help him through the grief. He's gonna be sad, and sometimes relieved, and a lot mad."

"I gotta go, but I promise I'll be there for him."

"Good."

Cassie hugged Annie in a soft hug.

"Need to take my meds and lie down."

She heard the weakness and breathiness in her friend's voice. Cassie pedaled fast as she left the Ingraham's. Several blocks from home her tears choked her so much she couldn't see. She stopped, got off her bike and wiped her face and nose.

"God, help me get through these coming weeks, my studying, finals, Christmas, Annie really going home."

෧

Cassie's a cappella group began the Holiday Fest in Hillyer's gym. Instead of being on the stage the singers stood behind and to the sides of the audience. She gazed around at the gym packed tight with spectators sitting in the bleachers on one side, and the floor of the gym filled with families and friends of the K-12 students. The young people sang, spoke and danced.

"They've made everything revolve around the song, *Joy to the World*, so beautifully done," Maggie turned and smiled to the parent on her right after the applause quieted from the presentation.

"Agree, ours is a second-grader; she's been seriously singing her number for weeks."

"My granddaughter's part of the a cappella group that began the concert. She mentioned there'd be audience participation, and there sure has been, great fun."

The two women nodded to each other as the next number started.

&

 "Grandma, please take this picture. I want to send to dad, to show him Luke."

Luke and Cassie stood before the Christmas tree in the great room.

"I'll snap two pictures, just in case."

They held hands as they made their way to the Holiday Ball in the Hillyer gym.

"Scared, I'm scared, Luke. Sheez, and I dance all the time without even thinking about it."

"Well, I've only been to one big dance like this before, so, hey," he paused and smiled to her before they went in, "we'll have fun, your grandma, coming to watch?"

"Yeah, she'll try to make it. My dress, it's because of her, I'd a never picked out one."

He squeezed her hand and looked into her blue eyes, "A beautiful dress for a beautiful young lady. I'm happy to be here with you."

Cassie felt her tears start as she listened to him.

"Hey, let's dance, a great fast one."

Luke twirled her again and again in the swing dance. They waltzed. Cassie looked up to the ceiling of the gym.

"Mom, I know you're watching me, this's somethin' I've dreamed of doing since my little girl days," her mind whirled.

Luke questioned her with his eyes.

She nodded, "Talkin' to mom," she whispered.

He smiled and they moved on, around and around the room in the waltz.

They sat out several dances at a table with a fellow student in Cassie's chem class and his girl.

"Got more energy now, the punch and cookies help," she smiled to Luke.

The other couple got up to dance.

"Kinda strange question, don't you have another set of grandparents, your mom's folks?"

"Uh huh, they're missionaries in Kenya. I only met them for the first time at mom's funeral. The rest of my life it's been letters and pictures."

"Missionaries, uh, you all are Catholic."

"Right, my mom converted to Catholicism before she married dad."

She looked into his eyes.

"I can hear what you're thinkin', yeah, her mom and dad weren't pleased, her being a preacher's kid and all. But she didn't care. God's God."

"Right."

During a fast swing Cassie glanced over to where an audience gathered to watch the dancers. She saw her tall, blonde grandma standing, in the back, with the other taller parents. When she could, she smiled and waved to Maggie.

"Grandma's here," she looked up to Luke as they began a slow dance."

"Sweet."

"Luke, I know you've got much on your mind," Cassie stood back from him as they stopped dancing a few dances later.

"I've had such a blast with you, Cassie."

"Me, too, but it's time to get me home. Thank you so much for this night."

She walked with him to her front porch, the outside porch light being on all night every night.

They hugged. He kissed her on top of her head.

"I'm so numb, Cassie, won't be myself for some time."

"I'll be right beside you, my spirit and yours, when we're not together, through this next time of your life. You're in my thoughts and prayers. I also pray for Annie."

She watched tears dribble down his cheeks as he nodded.

"I know."

He squeezed her hand and let go. She watched him as he stepped to his car in the driveway. She waved to him, and he waved back.

℘

In the Ingraham living room that same evening Ian and Annie danced several dances to a Christmas CD they picked together. Annie wore her light blue dress she had on for the Holiday Ball last year as a freshman.

"Exceedingly handsome, wow, you in a suit, Ian."

He presented her with a red carnation wrist corsage.

"Thank you," she bowed to him after he put it on her wrist.

He returned the bow and took her in his arms for the dance music they heard.

They sat together for a few minutes after they finished dancing several dances. During the last dance Annie stopped him.

"I'm feelin' so tired."

He swooped her up in his arms and danced and danced around the living room to the next two songs. He circled and circled.

"Dizzy," she giggled. He slowed and swayed until the music stopped.

"The fire, it's so homey, I love being near the tree and the fire, and near you, Ian."

She looked up into his eyes. Ian guided her head to his shoulder and held her in a hug.

"So we'll just stay here," he whispered, "maybe another dance?"

She moved her hand to his chest, "I, I don't think I can dance any more tonight. Please, let's just sit here in front of the fire."

Within 10 minutes Annie began to fall asleep. Jennifer Ingraham warned Ian this might happen. Ian called out to her. She came from the master bedroom upstairs.

"I'd like to carry her up, may I?"

Jennifer nodded to him as he gathered Annie in his arms and walked with care up the stairs to her bedroom. He helped her take off Annie's shoes after he lay her down on the bed. She covered her daughter with a light blanket and darkened the room.

They walked down the steps after Jennifer turned the hallway light on.

"She's just about finished with the semester, one more final to go for her. Her energy level's pretty much disappeared. Hospice will be visiting often. Please come and see Annie. She likes you so much."

Jennifer watched tears glaze Ian's eyes, "I love Annie," she heard him speak out.

"We'll all try to stay strong."

"We will."

She heard the determination as he spoke, "will."

Annie's dad walked Ian out to his pickup. Ian looked around at the multi-colored lights decorating the outside of Ingraham home.

"Son," he looked across to Ian, "we're so grateful you're in Annie's life. She's gotten to experience several different kinds of love in the last few months. Thank you for giving her this special time."

Ian nodded to Cliff Ingraham and held out his hand. They shook hands. Ian felt strength in Cliff's handshake.

80

"Finals, they're over," she shared with Miriam as Cassie walked into the vet clinic on the last day of school for that semester.

"Relieved?"

"Yeah, for reals, Hillyer's unlike any school I've been in. The discipline of studying'll help me wherever I end up in college."

As Maggie had asked her to, Cassie rode the bus from Hillyer to the Transit Center. She walked the few blocks to the clinic. Maggie got a call from the Ingraham's letting her know that Annie wanted to see Cassie. It would be for the last time. So Maggie wanted to drive her to the Ingraham home. She planned to visit for a few minutes with the family so Cassie and Annie could be together.

"No more pain, no more suffering, she's going to God," Cassie kept playing that tape again and again in her head.

The first thing she noticed was the special hospital bed Annie sat upright in. The bed positioned near the Christmas tree. A drip of medications attached to Annie's arm. She wore a bright red and green plaid pajama top and bottoms. Bunny rabbit slippers covered her feet.

Cassie smiled to her, "Finals done?"

She squeezed Annie's free hand.

"Yeah, finals're done. I had a good semester, what about you?"

"Excellent."

Annie raised her free arm and they high fived.

"They just added stuff to my drip, so I'll be resting in a couple of minutes. I'm so glad to see you, Cassie."

"For me to be with you," Cassie nodded to her.

"Talk about heaven, I hope it's comin' up soon for me. I'm goin' to God and to His angels, gonna be with them."

"You know we've talked about God and heaven."

"Yeah, God is love."

"Right."

"So ever' day, we love, we learn by loving, right Cassie?"

"That's right, Annie, I love you."

"And I love you, Cassie," she paused, "the deal is, you're gonna have lots more time to love, to learn by loving. You'll do that for me?"

Cassie nodded to her, "For the rest of my time, I'll keep learning how to love."

"Sleep's comin'. I c'n only imagine my future, only imagine. Cassie, hug me, please."

Cassie bent down as Annie raised up. They hugged. Cassie released her arms, and Annie lay back on the upright bed. She saw Annie's eyes close. The morphine took hold as Cassie stood for a moment watching her friend.

"Walk away, now, Cassie," she told herself.

She found her grandma sitting in the kitchen, having coffee with Annie's parents.

Cassie moved to the three of them.

"My mom's gone a year and a half. What helped me was being with people who'd suffered a recent loss in their lives. I'm gonna ask Emma, Luke, and Ian to join me in talking about what's happened to us with Annie. I think Ian's dad might be the adult to help us. He's a minister, been through this so many times."

"I'll get it set up, I know Revered Sjarlendone."

"Thanks, Grandma, it'll help us all."

Cassie looked around at the three of them.

"Dad went to counseling about my mom," she shifted her gaze from her grandma to Annie's folks, "I hope, sincerely, after things settle down in your lives, that you'll consider talking to someone."

"We will, you're so grown up, Cassie, what you've been through."

Cassie remembered; Luke and Annie's dad was a tax CPA.

"Yeah, oh, Mr. Ingraham, you got tax season, so maybe after that for you."

He smiled to Cassie and looked at Maggie, "She's amazing, is she not amazing?"

Maggie smiled back as the mood in the kitchen lightened, "Uh huh, she absolutely is."

They stood together in a group hug and said the Lord's Prayer.

Maggie held Cassie by the shoulder as they walked down the sidewalk to the van.

"GMag, I didn't say goodbye to Annie."

"Tell me."

"We hugged right before she went to sleep. All I could think of was," she paused, "until we meet again."

"That's it, Cassie, the way I feel about your granddad, until we meet again."

As they neared their home, Cassie's tears started.

"It's a whole bunch of stuff, finals over, Annie almost free of this life, for another life, same for mom and granddad, hoping and praying dad's safe."

"Cry it out Cassie, rest in your room, and we'll decide about the next days. You need a break and I'm taking off the day after Christmas. We'll plan a hike, do something active."

∾

Cassie joined her a cappella group as they sang Christmas carols in Pediatrics at Ephrine Memorial Hospital. She watched the delight on the children's faces, their eyes bright as they joined in with the caroling. The singers stood and sat with the children as they sang favorite carols. The group sang at several homes. They finished their singing at the Ingraham home, their last stop. Cassie especially requested they conclude their singing there. The carolers stood in the front yard as they hummed *Mary's Boy Child*. It was Annie's favorite Christmas song. The Ingraham family came out on their front porch.

Cassie saw Annie, wrapped in a blanket. Ian held her in his arms.

Cassie watched the desperation on Annie's lined face as she tried to smile to the group as they sang. Ian, Luke, and the parents joined in with the singing.

"I'm losin' it," Cassie thought as she stopped singing for a minute.

She felt the tears burn her eyes.

"Stop it, they need my voice, they all need my voice. This is for Annie."

Cassie regained control of her alto voice and blended it with the other singers for the final words of the song. "Silent Night" finished off their singing.

Annie raised her arm and waved to those gathered in front of her home.

The singers heard thank you's as they hummed, walking away from Annie's.

"Will I see her again in this life?"

Cassie asked herself that time and again as she got ready for bed that night. She prayed many Our Father's and Hail Mary's before she fell asleep.

&

Maggie knocked on Cassie's door, rousing her.

"I let you sleep in 'cause we got home in the early morning from midnight mass. Your dad's on the phone wishing us Merry Christmas."

Cassie took the call and filled her dad in on her holiday happenings.

"Stay strong, Cassie, your friend is going where pain and suffering, well you know, are no longer there. Be happy for her, like we were with mom."

"How do I do it, Dad?"

"Take it," he paused, "uh, like we did, one hour at a time, one day at a time, 'specially when she's gone to God."

"OK, Dad, I'll stay strong. For the second year it just doesn't feel like Christmas, the last one, well after mom. And this one, with Annie. They'll let us know when Annie goes home, to her real home. I'm gonna enjoy the time off 'cause we begin classes on Monday after the New Year, on the 4th. Dad?"

"What, dear one?"

"My PSAT scores, really good, guess it didn't hurt that I was in so many different schools growing up."

"Just did what we asked."

"Yeah, 'do your best, Cassie, take advantage of every opportunity,' that's what you and mom kept telling me, from Pre-K on."

The phone went silent.

"Talk to me, Cassie."

"Gonna have a little group of us get together to talk about being sad, and mad, and someday maybe glad when we lose Annie. Grandma's gonna help get us set up with a minister. My special friend, Luke, is gonna be a part of it. Annie is his sister."

"Good girl."

"Dad, you haven't shared."

"Can't tell you, except I like what I'm doing, a lot of traveling, and most important, I'm getting some happiness back. That's my hope for you as the next months go by, be happy, you got so much good going on in your life."

"Merry Christmas, Dad, I'll put grandma on now. I love you."

"And I love you, Cassie."

∛

"I haven't even asked, Grandma, what about Christmas dinner? I didn't feel like opening presents this morning, just wanted to have hot chocolate with you. I gotta get a handle on all this; I'm forgetting everyone in my life, all the important people. I been too focused on me."

Maggie poured each of them a little more hot chocolate as they sat together at the breakfast nook.

"I just mentioned it briefly; we're going to Brad's for Christmas dinner, at 2 p.m. He and his girlfriend cooked a turkey breast and the rest of the fixings. I'm bringing pumpkin pie and whipped topping. And Cassie, Brad's dad is joining us. He's also a veterinarian, knew Steph from regional vet meetings. He's thinking of at least partially retiring soon."

Cassie nodded her head to her grandma.

"Couple things I need to do, Grandma, and then I'll get ready."

Cassie trudged up the steps; each foot felt lead heavy. Then it hit her. She sat down hard at the top of the stairs.

"My grandma, she needs love in her life, uh, I wonder, this vet I'll meet, somebody for my GMag?"

Then she shook her head as a second thought struck her, "Cassie, you are a hopeless romantic, always looking for love for folks. But wouldn't it be nice for my grandma to find someone in her very busy life?"

Cassie bounced up from the stair and headed to get ready.

"I'm gonna really check this guy out," she announced out loud as she brushed her hair.

She saw herself in the mirror, a little smile making her feel more in the holiday spirit. She hummed *Mary's Boy Child* and thought of Annie for just a moment.

As Cassie walked up the driveway to Brad's place with her grandma, Maggie stopped her.

"Have fun, enjoy the food and conversation. This day, it's an important day, it's all we got, Cassie."

Cassie put her arm around her grandma's shoulder, "I know it is, I'll try."

"I'm having fun," she told herself as they all paused, giving everyone a little time before dessert got served.

She watched the interaction of her grandma and Brad's dad, Dave. Cassie got the impression that they knew each other during some past time in their lives. But hey, it was none of her business. She tried to imagine him replacing her granddad. She couldn't do that; not enough time passed since her granddad left his family.

That evening when they got home Cassie and her grandma exchanged presents. Cassie smiled as Maggie expressed surprise at the stethoscope she received from her granddaughter.

They laughed together, "You've even noticed it, my absentmindedness in keeping track of the darn thing. I used to be better about wearing it around my neck, but I kinda got out of the habit. I'll start doing that again. I'm really happy I've got a spare one, just in case."

"For reals, this is the best, my favorite present, thanks dad," Cassie held the textbook close. "I'll read it from cover to cover."

She showed the book to Maggie, "I'm finally old enough to begin to understand microbiology, I've asked and asked for four years. I know you got it for dad to give me, thanks, Grandma."

Cassie paused, and hugged her grandma, "Thank you for this very nice day."

That night Cassie began to fall asleep, in the calm of her mind she again accepted God's being in charge.

She and her grandma headed out early that Saturday, the day after Christmas, to hike in the hills an hour away from Ephrine. Maggie gave her office staff a day off so everyone could enjoy a weekend of three days with no time in the clinic. Cassie asked that the hike and getting away be the Christmas present from her grandma.

℃

Cassie picked up the phone the next morning. They were almost out the door to early mass in a few minutes. She heard Luke's husky voice.

"She's with God and His angels, Cassie."

The lump in her throat ached and ached as it enlarged. Tears blinded her eyes.

Cassie choked out, "I'm so sorry, let your folks know too. Is there anything me and grandma can do?"

"We're having a celebration of her life day after tomorrow, here, at noon, wear blue, Annie's favorite color. Our family really wants you and Maggie to come."

"Does Emma know?"

"Yeah, she and her parents will be here."

"So will we. I've prayed so much for you and your dad and mom. I'll continue to do that. I know peoples' prayers got me and dad through those first days. There's no way anybody can prepare for the loss," she paused, "no way, Luke?"

4

"What's that, Cassie?"

"I'll walk, right beside you, in these next days, in your sad times, mad times, and one day, glad times."

"Thank you, Cassie."

"You know I care about you, Luke."

"I know."

She hung up the phone as her grandma walked up to her. Cassie shook her head. They hugged each other. Cassie cried as they drove to church. Maggie held her hand as they walked into St. Luke's. She brightened as she viewed the long row of red poinsettias along the front sanctuary.

She could not concentrate on the service. A tape played over and over in her head, "No more pain, no more suffering, you're home, Annie."

Cassie watched the smiling congregation file out of church on that glorious blue sky morning. She regained the peace she felt on Christmas night.

&

30 invited guests sat and stood in the Ingraham great room, dining area and kitchen. Cliff Ingraham made his way to the

front of the fireplace. He looked around at the crowd, smiled to everyone and began.

"Annie told us that everyone needed to eat hearty at her celebration. Uh huh, she planned a lot of this when she was able. So, per her instructions we've had folks prepare lots of chow, her favorites for you to enjoy. And thanks for wearing blue, her favorite color, her sky blue eyes."

He choked for a moment.

"Annie wanted research done. Often ALL is completely curable. But in her case, some anomaly kept her only in remission until the last few months. Per her wishes," he put up his hand, looked up to the ceiling, and smiled, helping everyone to smile, "her body's been donated to research. This is happening at a children's research hospital in Memphis, TN."

He nodded to the group, "She's already been taken there, and her firm hope is that she will have some small part in finding a cure for cancer. Annie had a favorite saint, Teresa of Avila. She wanted St. Teresa's words expressed at her celebration. St. Teresa's words guided Annie."

"Let nothing disturb you. Let nothing frighten you, all things are passing away: God never changes. Patience obtains all things. Whoever has God lacks nothing; God alone suffices."

Luke stood next to Cassie.

She held his hand, stood on tiptoe and whispered in his ear, "That's so totally outa sight, Luke, totally Annie."

He looked down into her eyes, "Someday, maybe I'll be a part of that research. For sure, I'm hoping I'll work in Pediatrics."

Cliff concluded, "Annie wished for you all to hear two of her favorite songs, "The Dance," Garth Brooks, and Whitney Houston's "I Will Always Love You." So here they are as you gather to chow down, please enjoy."

"The food's delicious, and the music, it lifts my spirits," Annie's parents heard that comment from many of the folks gathered to celebrate Annie.

Cassie moved among the people before she got in the food line. She chatted with some she knew, including their dance instructor, Ian, and Emma. Emma took Cassie to her parents for introductions.

"Mom and Dad, this is Cassie."

"I'm Denise," she shook Cassie's hand.

"And I'm Sam," he smiled to her as he shook her hand. "Emma talks about you a lot, you dance together, right?"

"Uh huh, I'm a fellow dancer in the group," she nodded. "It's good to meet you. Have you met my grandma, Maggie Montclare?"

"Oh yes," Denise spoke up, "she's our vet, a very special lady, saved the life of one of our dear little dogs."

Emma and Cassie walked away from her parents and helped themselves to dessert.

"How're you doing Emma, you guys been friends for a long time?"

"Yeah, we've been, but it changed when Annie transferred to Hillyer. We weren't able to see each other much, except weekends, for dance class."

"I hope we can continue our friendship, get together as much as we can."

"Cassie, I sure hope so. You're carrying such a load at Hillyer; you have to study so much more than I do. That bothers me sometimes."

"If you're happy with your classes and your teachers, that's what matters, Emma, OK?"

Emma nodded.

"We'll get together to help us with Annie, right?"

"Uh huh, Reverend Sjarlendone's gonna help."

"Isn't that Ian's dad?"

"Yeah."

"I'm so sad right now; I want to go home. Did you have a good Christmas?"

"I did, under the circumstances."

They hugged, and Cassie found her grandma. They made sure they thanked the Ingrahams. Luke and Cassie hugged at his front door.

"I care, Cassie."

"And I care, be good to yourself."

He nodded to her.

She watched his face, his red-veined eyes, so tired looking. It was the saddest she ever saw him.

&

"It was so lovely, Cassie, so what Annie wanted, her folks told me."

"Yeah," she looked over to her grandma as they drove home, "her dad mentioned that several times."

"Grandma?"

"Yes, hon?"

"Sure surprised when I met Emma's folks. They're black. Emma looks very much like her mom, in the face. But Emma's got blue-green eyes. Is she adopted?"

"She's not, Cassie, she is their biological daughter. They have an older son, away at college. He's helped bring in their dogs, years back, to the clinic. He's black."

"Uh, so there's gotta be someone white in Emma's background, like a great grandparent or something. Her skin is lighter than mine, and I'm blonde. And her hair, such a lovely light brown. Uh, actually that's none of my darn business."

Maggie turned to her granddaughter.

"From what I know of the family, it's a parent on Emma's mom's side."

"Wow, Grandma, is it a blessing or a curse for Emma?"

"Both, I think. "

"Genetics, sheez, crazy, aren't they?"

"They are."

80

Cassie sat cross-legged in front of the Christmas tree after she turned on the tree lights. Maggie left Cassie at home and went directly to the clinic. She had several appointments late that afternoon.

"God," Cassie spoke out, "I've lost a special friend, Annie. She's with mom, in my heart, close by. But I have another friend, Emma. All I can do about Emma is what I always do with those I care for, just love that person. I hope she gets treated like the child of God that she is. Projecting ahead, and I do that too much, I think she may have it pretty tough, when she goes away to school, to explain who she is. Friends are color blind, right?"

God didn't answer her question, not that night, and not in the next days.

80

"Can I come over on my bike? I'm missing Annie, but I'm missing you too."

"Hey, Luke, glad you called, been moping around, got chores done, but I just don't even feel like reading. I've got Christmas mail to open, just can't do it right now. Yeah, we'll go bike riding. I sure need the exercise, actually I ran this morning, in the neighborhood. It felt good for a little while. Then a big old wave of sadness smacked me."

15 minutes later Luke arrived.

"Yeah," he said after he gave her a hug, "waves of sadness, hey that's a good way to think about it, smack me too."

They headed out in their light jackets, bike helmets on. They rode and rode, on residential streets, away from the busy downtown area. Cassie signaled for him to stop.

"Can we walk our bikes for a bit?"

"Course."

"I'm back in school on Monday."

"Me too, New Year's Day's tomorrow. Do you have plans for tonight?"

"Nope, just a quiet evening with grandma; she hates being out on the roads on a night like this."

"Yeah, my folks, they're completely exhausted. I helped them clear Annie's room of her stuff. She donated her body, but she's also giving away all but the smallest of her possessions."

"Uh huh, she mentioned that people needed her stuff. She wanted to make sure her room became a guest bedroom. It needs to be used she said; 'didn't want mom and dad to make my room into a shrine, ick, no way.'"

"Wow, that's so Annie, yup, she's always been a giver, kind hearted to everyone."

"She understood, early on, about how to treat people, like it was a gift she had."

"It was, Cassie," he paused, "Uh."

Luke stopped walking his bike and pulled to the far right side of a sidewalk near the park.

"Annie, there's something she wanted to give you. You don't wear a watch, so she thought of it. She told me what she had in mind; I bought it for her. She said I needed to give it to you, but not until a few days after she went home. She approved, got a big smile on her face when I showed it to her."

Luke handed Cassie a red tissue paper present from his jacket pocket. Cassie parked her bike behind his and began to open the tissue. She felt her cold hands tremble as she burst into tears.

"But I didn't give her anything."

Her tears dropped on the tissue.

"Uh huh, yes you did, you shared your time with her, and you gave her love. She loved you, Cassie, just as I love you."

Through her tears Cassie tried to look at the bracelet. She held it closer and saw a small golden heart with small diamonds, one next to the bottom of the heart and one above the top of the heart.

"It's so lovely, thank you, Annie," Cassie whispered

"I showed it to her after I got it. She said it was you, Cassie, simple and classic."

"That's me," she nodded as she raised her tear-stained eyes to him.

He broke into tears as they hugged and cried together. He helped her put it on her wrist.

Luke held her arm up, as if showing Annie the bracelet, "What do ya think, Sis?"

Neither of them spoke, half expecting Annie to reply. They paused, then shook their heads to each other.

"Gosh, thanks for taking the time to get the bracelet for me; how did you do it all, school, helping your folks, you took over the care of your doggy, right?"

"I did; I stepped up. And you know what?"

Cassie moved back away from him.

"What, Luke?"

"This fall semester I made the best grades I've ever made in my life. That's 'cause I got super focused. I learned time management."

"Yeah, I learned to break my homework and studying into 30 minute sessions. Pretty amazing what a person can accomplish in 30 minutes, if they need to."

"30 and 30 and 30, I'll try those time chunks this semester."

"Hey Luke, should I say congrats on your grades?"

"Uh huh, only one B, what about you?"

"All A's."

They high fived and headed back to Cassie's.

"Happy New Year, Luke."

"Same, Cassie."

She watched him pedal away after they hugged. Her tears started after she could no longer see him.

"God bless and keep the Ingraham family," she cried out.

ℵ

Cassie watched it rain and rain that January. Her mood reflected the continual gray of the days.

Before dance class started each Saturday she would share with Emma, "Rain's our tears comin' down from holes in the floor of heaven."

They always hugged. And by the time dance class finished, both of them felt better, happier. They decided that exercise, by itself, worked to help them be more positive.

Cassie tried out for a dance part in a community play to be presented in March. It didn't work out for her, though, because practices took serious time away from her studies in the evenings. Second semester AP Chem and the calculus class kept her super busy. One early Saturday morning she took out the Christmas mail she just didn't feel like opening over the holidays.

"Cassie, you sit right here at your desk and answer these letters back. Explain what's going on."

She opened Mia's card first. As she read through the Christmas card and enclosed note, she began to laugh. Mia explained a couple of antics she pulled off during the fall semester at Smith High, Cassie's high school last year.

"It, wow, was super cool that I got to know Mia. She brightened every life she touched," Cassie murmured as she remembered the bouncy spirited redhead. "And, of course, she's a cheerleader."

Cassie wrote Mia, vowing to get the card out in the Monday morning mail. She looked at the cheerful card with different colored roses on the cover.

"I tried to be as positive as I could be," she nodded as she addressed the envelope.

She used Mia's letter as a guide to write cards back to her grandparents in Kenya and her other friend at Smith High. With each letter she enclosed a school picture. All the pictures she took during the fall were group shots, always including Annie. She decided she just couldn't send one of those.

"There hasn't been enough time," she shook her head as she took the letters to the place off the kitchen where they kept outgoing mail before they took it out to the mailbox.

&

"I'm liking our talks about Annie, about loss," she shared after the third visit Ian, Emma, Luke, and Cassie had with Reverend Sjarlendone.

From that time forward Reverend suggested they meet one-on-one with him, when they felt the need. The group agreed. Emma and Luke concluded they still wanted to see Reverend. Ian and Cassie each spoke up about not knowing Annie for as long a period of time as the other two had. Each teen could make his or her own decision.

&

Luke and Cassie continued with CYO. He picked her up the three Sundays of the month that the group met and took her home after they attended church together.

Father Paul's constant message to the CYO group, "Believe, believe in yourself. You have many life decisions coming up in the next couple of years. Believe."

In early February Maggie asked Luke to stay for a Sunday noon meal with Cassie and her after church. Cassie made chocolate chip bars, to take home for his parents and him.

"Wanted to just check in with you, Luke," Maggie said during the meal.

"Maggie, I'm sad, but each day I feel a little better. My folks reminded me that College Boards are coming up. And I need to really think about colleges, and in just a few months, applying."

"Luke, you're an extremely fast runner. And Cassie, you haven't seen him play soccer yet."

She smiled to her granddaughter.

"He's absolutely superb."

Cassie shook her head, "You've never said a word, about practicing or about anything connected with soccer. You play?"

"Goalie, for Ephrine High and fill in occasionally for an injured player. I do like to run."

He grinned to them, and shook his head, "'Cept nobody wants to play goalie, so I'm it. Once in a while I get a good run in, during a game, uh, substituting."

"Cassie, he's fearless."

Cassie looked from her grandma to Luke, "I'd a never guessed that; I got a lot to learn about you!"

"Yeah, you do, I'm just kinda quiet around folks."

"But not out on the soccer field, I would encourage you, if you have not, to really try for an athletic scholarship to a university, hey with your speed and your no fear attitude. Your cross country team is fast, too."

Maggie nodded to Luke as she smiled to him.

"I take it you've watched Luke play soccer a bit."

"Uh huh, I have, Kay Ann, you know my tech at the clinic, has a son."

"Yeah, Kent and me, well since before first grade we played in the city's soccer league. Then we joined a soccer group that had super high expectations. But I like playing soccer with my high school, that's the best, 'cause we travel out of town some for competitions with other high schools."

"Uh, Kent, still playing with you?"

"Nah, he kept growing taller and heftier, so he plays football for Ephrine High."

He got up, and Cassie touched his arm.

"Gotta head out, homework, housework, our family sorta has a schedule finally. Mom and I do most 'cause dad's got taxes, super huge until after April 15. Maggie, could I like talk private with you for a minute? It's a little family matter; Cassie, won't share with you, just need advice, you got a wise grandma."

Luke hugged Cassie. She handed him the bag of chocolate chip bars. He nodded to her and smiled.

"I heard from one college, Luke."

"And?"

"The banner wasn't there's; the librarian did do some checking and suggested another school, but it's in Mississippi."

"There'll be more letters coming your way."

She nodded, "I know," she paused and let out a big breath, "patience."

Maggie and Luke stood outside for a moment on the porch, then walked together to his car.

"I talked to Reverend, but I need your advice. Mom and dad, they're fighting, big time, verbal stuff, Annie's death, it's opened up a lot of feelings that I guess got suppressed for years."

"Well, Luke, I c'n just relate my experiences in the world of pets with grief. Neglect, I see pets neglected after deaths of humans. I see pets that get fought over, injured sometimes when people work on their emotions. Pray for your folks. Luke, know that the death of a child sometimes creates difficulties in a marriage, sure have seen that some, in our community. Fortunately, college comes along soon for you. And, of course, love your mom and dad and continue to help out as you have. You gotta be strong, 'cause they aren't right, uh themselves, now, nor may be for some time. Remember, you have your own life to live."

"Thank you, Maggie, you're advice, good, important."

"You could use a hug."

Maggie came to him and they hugged.

"Thanks, I really needed that. And Maggie, I really really care about Cassie."

"I know, and I know that you have a great deal going on in your life, with school and sports and your folks. Again I say make time for you, please."

"I'll try, thank you for listening to me."

ℂ

"I want to celebrate Valentine's Day with you, GMag. Neither Luke nor I are ready to be anything more than friends who love each other right now."

"Maybe would you like to invite Emma to dinner to celebrate with the two of us?"

"Gosh, hadn't thought about that."

They looked at their calendars that morning and found several dates that might work besides the actual day. Cassie stopped by the clinic, just decided to do that on her own, after school that day. They closed the clinic and were about ready to leave. The phone rang. Miriam just left for the evening, so Cassie picked up the call. It was Brad. Earlier in the day he needed to look in on an injured horse at the Cloverdale Stables. Cassie handed the phone to Maggie.

Cassie watched Maggie nod her head as she listened to her partner. Her grandma grabbed a pencil and paper and began writing down information.

When she hung up, she turned to Cassie, "I'll need your help; Brad's still out at the stables; you'll come along and assist. I need to take these meds. Please read them to me from the list after I unlock the meds cabinets."

Cassie tried to read the names of the several almost unpronounceable drugs. Her grandma understood, and together they assembled what they would need to take.

"I'm not sure what we're facing, Cassie. I'll explain, oh gosh, you'll see for yourself. Leave your backpack here, we'll pick it up on the way back, and quick, change from your uniform into those jeans and sweat shirt you keep here, when you help out."

"Yeah, my grandma in action," she smiled to Maggie as they drove away from the clinic.

Cassie watched the winter landscape pass them by; stark naked trees, brown ground, and some pine trees scattered along the small hills as they neared the stables. She remembered riding a pony here during one of her summer outings with her grandparents when she was younger.

"It's much worse than I imagined, Maggie," Brad looked up to her from the barn floor where he knelt, working on the horse.

"Come closer."

Cassie watched as Maggie knelt beside Brad. They continued to work together to untangle the barbed wire wrapped around the horse's feet. Two other people stood away from where the injured horse lay. They wore baseball caps pulled low.

Brad whispered to her, "This's on purpose, no other way the horse could'a got so entangled. What in the hell is going on out here?"

He shook his head as he and Maggie worked together to remove the barbed wire, staunch the bleeding and then stitch up the horse's wounds. Out of the corner of her eye Cassie watched the observers turn and walk away from them, in slow-like motion. With gloved hands she carefully took the bloodied barbed wire and removed it to the outside of the barn. It took her three trips to get all the wire outside.

She returned to watch as Brad and Maggie coaxed the horse back up on its feet. The horse staggered, kept whinnying and shaking. Cassie saw it stay upright.

"Water, Cassie please get us some water for the horse."

She ran to the water trough with a bucket, filled it just enough so that she could carry it back.

"Oops, good grief," she shouted out as she slopped the precious water out of the bucket onto her legs.

She set the bucket down for the horse to drink. Brad and Maggie began to put away their medical equipment and supplies. Cassie turned and stepped out of the stall. She smelled the acrid odor. Then she glimpsed a horse jumping up and down and screaming as flames licked up the low wood of the horse stall.

"Fire," she screamed out, "the end of the stable's on fire. Grandma, your mobile phone?"

"In the van, go, make the call. We gotta get the horses out."

After she made the call, she ran back inside the barn. The vets had masks over their noses and mouths. Maggie handed her one. Brad and Maggie coaxed the injured horse out of the stall. The filly limped so badly that Cassie thought it would fall down.

"Let 'em out, Cassie," Brad called out to her.

Cassie went from stall to stall opening the doors, trying to move out the horses. Some came willingly and others cowered in the corner of the stalls. She kept the mask over her mouth and nose. But now her eyes burned from the smoke. Tears almost blinded Cassie's eyes as she squinted, watching Brad and Maggie run ahead to the stalls farther into the stables.

"Dear God, help them, those stalls are on fire. The horses gonna burn up."

Something made her pause. Then ahead she saw bales of hay, on fire, fall from the edge of the barn attic onto the dirt floor of the barn.

She heard a voice, her mom's voice, "Cassie, come away, come away."

"Where did that come from?" Cassie questioned, speaking into the sweat-filled mask.

She stepped back and tripped on something on the ground behind her. She fell hard, onto the floor. That stunned her for a moment. Then she turned over and began crawling on her stomach, hand over hand over hand. Her dizziness started to overtake her. She made it to the outside of the large open barn door. She kept crawling after she tore the mask away from her face.

"Air," she breathed and breathed in the cleaner air. After a time she heard sirens approaching. The sky darkened as she looked up and turned her head to her left side.

She raised up two fingers on her right hand. The fireman got close to her as she croaked out, "Two people inside, save."

As the fireman turned her over on her back, she fainted.

&

Cassie felt something pressing against her face. She squinted as she tried to open her eyes.

"It's a mask, feels like it's smothering me," she spoke out as her left hand removed it.

She took deep breaths, a couple of them making her lungs ache. She turned her head from side to side.

"Must be an emergency room," she looked up at the lights and saw all sorts of medical equipment nearby. A device held her finger, and she looked at the saline bag attached to her right arm.

"Hi Cassie."

"Kay Ann."

"Where's grandma and Brad?"

"Taken to rooms."

"So, serious."

"Uh huh, smoke inhalation, much more than what you were exposed to."

"Burns?"

"Minor."

"Nuthin second or third?"

"Nope."

"Your grandma's gonna need a new haircut and style, one side of her head, the hair, got singed bad."

"Can I sit up more?"

"Sure."

Kay Ann raised the top of the bed up so Cassie could see better.

An ER nurse showed up and checked on Cassie's readings. Cassie told her she felt pretty good, considering.

"Tell me, Kay Ann, how bad was it?"

"Firemen are considering the stable a total loss."

"Horses?"

"Five died; seven saved."

"Kay Ann, what about the two observers?"

"Found them, under arrest, Brad's got the goods on those people."

"Arson?"

"Uh huh, and charges brought regarding you three, you all coulda died out there."

"Kay Ann?"

"Yeah, honey?

"Mom, my mom, she's with God, well, she spoke to me as the firey hay bales fell down from the attic in front of me. I heard her say 'Cassie, come away, come away.' And I did, I stepped back and tripped on something on the ground and I went down. That's why I had to crawl out of the barn, couldn't get up to save myself."

"We're so proud of you."

"Uh, what'd I do?"

"You saved four of the horses."

"Wow, I did? It all happened so fast, a flurry of animals getting away."

"Your grandma and Brad saved the other three, but the others didn't make it."

"Tell me."

"Horribly burned and fried lungs, they were put down."

"I'm so sorry."

Within an hour Cassie got released from the ER. She found her way to the Medical wing with Kay Ann to visit her grandma and Brad.

She held her grandma's hand as Cassie looked her over.

"I know, I know, granddaughter, I'll be lots better when I get cleaned up."

"You're OK, that's what matters. They gonna keep you overnight?"

"Yes, but I get to come home tomorrow. I have my beautician coming to figure out what to do with my hair."

"I know you like it shoulder length, GMag, but it'll have to be cut short."

"Knew you'd say that, it'll work, right Kay Ann?"

"Right, boss."

"What about the office tomorrow, Grandma?"

"It'll all be rearranged. Kay Ann will take you home."

"I'll be fine for tonight and for school tomorrow. God's been with us tonight, every step of the way."

Cassie paused, remembering.

"Your van, grandma?"

"Not to worry, both Brad's and my vehicle will be back in their parking spots behind the clinic by tomorrow afternoon."

"I love you, Cassie, thanks for all you did to help."

She hugged Maggie.

"I'll come to the clinic after school."

"Good, see you then."

Cassie dropped in to Brad's room. He thanked her for helping them and assured her he would be back in the office the next afternoon. On the way home Cassie talked about flashbacks she knew she would have from the incident at the stables. Kay Ann came in to the darkened home with Cassie. She carried Cassie's backpack.

"I heard your grandma ask that you leave your backpack at the clinic. I stopped by and picked it up."

"Thank you so much for remembering, I'll get up real early and get as much homework done as I can. It's so wonderful that you understand what a load I carry."

"I certainly do, good night Cassie, you are one lucky young lady," she nodded to her.

Cassie closed the front door after Kay Ann left. She remembered the front porch light.

&

She tossed and turned all that night. In a panic she woke up. When she saw that it was 5 a.m., she blew out a breath of relief.

"Get downstairs, make coffee, do as much as you can before school."

Cassie remembered then the words Kay Ann spoke to her as she left the Montclare home last night.

Kay Ann hugged her and whispered, "You're part of our family, Cassie, you and your grandma, not just the medical part, but you two, are in our hearts also."

Cassie took a sip of her coffee as her tears came, "People care, they do." She proceeded to finish as much homework as she could before she walked to the Transit Center for her bus. That day she skipped lunch. She studied in the far end of the library, eating a snack, almost catching up.

ℂ

"Grandma, I'm so relieved that you're OK and back to the clinic."

"Pretty awesome, how you helped us."

They hugged, and Cassie stepped back from her grandma.

"Your stylist did a really fine job with your haircut."

"Now I just gotta grow my hair out. I really dislike it being short."

"Did you get to rest at home for a little while?"

"I did, with a thorough shower, and I threw away the smoke-damaged clothes I was wearing. You should probably do the same."

"Yeah, I'll put spare clothes at the clinic that I can change into from my school uniform."

"Cassie, an arson investigator will be here in a few minutes to take down information about what you saw happen at the stables."

Cassie sat in a back office doing homework when the investigator showed up. She answered his questions, and the man left after 15 minutes. Kay Ann shooed Cassie and her grandma out of the office after the last appointment finished.

"How about breakfast for dinner?"

They both agreed as Maggie drove into the garage. They gave each other 45 minutes to make some order again in their lives. After they ate, Maggie lay down.

"My shortness of breath, kinda scares me, it keeps coming back every time I try to exert myself."

Cassie hugged her grandma, "I'll keep an eye on you."

Cassie decided to work at the dining room table on her homework that evening. She answered the phone.

"Cassie, wow, you're in the paper, are you guys OK?"

"Uh huh, grandma and Brad had some serious smoke inhalation, but they'll hopefully be better every day. They gotta try to take it a little easy, you know, their lungs. The docs just kept them overnight at the hospital, doin' respiratory stuff."

"You, how're you?"

"Luke, I'm hangin in there, but I'll have some sleep issues for a while. I'm just super tired, hope that'll help me sleep."

"You're hoarse, Cassie."

"Yeah, that's part of the smoke inhalation problem."

"I want to come and see you."

"Uh, probably won't work out, maybe Saturday, after dance class."

"I know you have tons of homework, but I miss seeing you, except Sundays which I really look forward to."

"Thanks for checking in on us."

"I care, so much, Cassie," she heard his voice grow husky.

"You're missing Annie, too, your voice."

"Right, see you soon."

∮

Emma joined Maggie and Cassie for a Valentine lunch later in February. It gave Cassie and her grandma a chance to recover from the stable fire. Maggie decided to have the lunch at their favorite café downtown on Saturday afternoon.

"Dance recital, ladies?"

Emma shared the plan the dance group had for the district presentation they would make in Macon. If they won that, the group would head to Atlanta for a state dance recital.

"It's modern dance, pretty creative; we've been practicing since after the holidays, including all the dance movements that we'll be tested on."

"Are you ready?"

Both teens nodded to Maggie.

After they ate and were digging into their dessert of hot fudge sundaes, Maggie looked from one to the other.

"To start with, Cassie, it's gonna be really important that you learn to drive, and soon. I would like you not to have to take a bus to Hillyer your last two years. So I've done some checking, with your parents, Emma."

"Uh huh, they said something about driving to me."

"It seems that you both have June birthdays and that you're old enough now to go to driving school, also to get your provisional license."

"Would we, could we, Grandma, could I go to driving school?"

"Certainly, Emma's folks would like you and Emma to partner and take the classes together."

"Saturday afternoons?"

"Uh huh, the driving school I have in mind has some openings for the Saturday p.m. class."

Emma and Cassie looked at each other and grabbed hands.

"Totally special, after dance class, we'd have time, that'll really fill up our Saturdays."

"Grandma, it's something I have to do," Cassie said in a solemn tone, nodding to Maggie.

"Uh, I guess my folks are on board?"

"They are, Emma."

"We'll go get our provisionals and get going, riding with an adult."

"So, that would mean that not too long after we turn 16, provided we pass the course and all the tests they have, uh, and the state tests we could start driving?"

"Wow, on your own."

"What about wheels?" Cassie turned to Emma.

"My parents have my brother's car parked next to our two car garage. No one drives it, but they keep the plates and insurance up."

"Why isn't he driving it?"

"Cause, Cassie, he's at a school where wheels are a real hindrance, an old pain in the butt."

"So you'd have a car to drive?"

"Uh huh, at least through a part of my senior year. By then, who knows."

"Cassie, have you not wondered about granddad's little pickup in the garage?"

"No, not really."

"Well, it'll be for you to drive."

"Wow, for reals, GMag?"

Maggie noticed the very surprised look on Cassie's face and nodded, "For reals."

"Thank you, Maggie, you've done a ton of leg work for Cassie, and for me, contacting my parents."

"It's a very important next phase of your lives, being able to get around, because parents work. We're unable to take you some places because of our jobs."

"Grandma, I've gotten really creative about getting places. It's been good for me, to have to figure out how to get somewhere either walking, or riding my bike, or taking the city bus. So if it works out, before long I'll have a bit of freedom."

Maggie saw their smiles, Cassie giving her the signature wide smile she always had from little girlhood, and Emma's sweet smile.

℃

"It's my best present ever," she looked over to Maggie as Cassie drove her to the clinic, on that very dog day of the hot and humid Georgia summer.

"And it's so nice to be able to have transportation while the van's in the shop, Cassie."

After she left her grandma off at the clinic, she headed home to wash her granddad's pickup, hers now. She used a soapy bucket of warm water and a sponge to remove the pollen grime. She sprayed the pickup off with the cool water and wiped it down with an old towel.

"A year," she spoke out, "I've been at grandma's a whole year. Spring semester, great, gosh college boards coming up after school starts. Oh Annie, my memory of you's starting to fade."

She looked down, at her right arm. She'd forgotten to wear Annie's bracelet, now for several days. She nodded, "Annie, will you understand? You wanted so much for me to have the bracelet."

ℂ

"We're so excited; I hope you'll let me help Cassie out."

The Ingraham's sat at their breakfast nook. Jennifer poured lemonade for Luke's dad, Cassie, Luke, and herself.

"Thank you for bringing the chocolate chip bars, Luke raves," Jennifer laughed as she nodded to her son.

"Lay it all out, kids. We know you've done some work on this."

"The banner Cassie's granddad had, we researched, Cassie, Annie, and I have. We wrote letters to 11 different schools."

"So Granddad Montclare's request, we're gonna fulfill it. We found the school where it belongs."

"It'll be kind'a big deal."

Cassie went on to explain as she laid the picture out on the table for his parents to see.

"Here's the banner, this picture doesn't do it justice, but on the top of the banner, in small lettering is the word Cooper's, which is hard to see. And there was a piece of paper attached, with two rusty straight pins, that said Return to and then the rest was unreadable, except for 192 and then the last number, couldn't read it.

"Hawks, the banner's got nice lettering for the word."

"Yeah, mom and dad, it's a good banner, had to have been expensive from that era."

"We heard back from 10 of the 11 schools. I have all the letters saved, in a binder, I love doing research, and this's been so fun."

"So, we want to drive to Altanhoot, it's a city in southwest Georgia. There's a small university there, the University of Triberiar. The banner belongs to that school, but now their mascot is harriers, not hawks."

Cassie took over, "Mrs. Sarison, my letter landed on her desk. She's part of the library staff at the university. And she's an avid historian. She couldn't get to our request for a bit because of a project she'd been charged with by the school's president."

Luke's dad nodded.

"So when she could, she dug in, and learned that the mascot changed."

"Uh huh, it took a bit to uncover that info. She got help from the athletic department."

"Yeah, mom and dad, the university had, what today would be a Division III football team in the 1920's. Things got so rough, the economy, that the team got disbanded during the depression. And athletics didn't really get established again until the late 30's, and then the war came along. But by the end of 1945 the school, like many in our country, started filling up with World War II veterans. So athletics got really revived, among the programs the return of Division III, small school football."

They paused, drinking down the rest of their glasses of lemonade. Cassie smiled to Luke and nodded to his parents.

"Luke's helped me, on several nights this summer, write letters of thanks to the staffs from the nine schools who gave us information that it wasn't their banner. We shared our findings with them."

"So the university's asked for their old banner back. And we want to comply. Mrs.Sarison's gonna host us for the evening that we're there, have us spend the night at her home, feed us breakfast, and then send us back."

"Oh, the athletic director and the football coach want to meet us the afternoon we arrive with the banner. Mrs. Sarison says that they have information to share with us."

Cassie paused, "I really hope you'll let Luke come with me. He'd miss two cross country practices."

The parents looked from Cassie to Luke, and Luke's dad spoke up.

"Absolutely, we'll let Luke go with you; this is exciting news, fulfilling a request your granddad had, Cassie. As a matter of fact, I'm giving Luke my car to drive for the trip. His car's older, not quite as reliable."

Jennifer shook her head, "There's a question that hasn't been answered."

Both Luke and Cassie nodded, "Yeah, we know, how the heck did granddad get hold of the banner? Granddad gave my dad serious instructions about returning the banner to its rightful owner. But."

Cassie fell silent for a bit, "But," she shook her head, "he never shared with dad the circumstances, only to return it."

"Embarrassed, do you think, about how it all went down, how he got it?"

"Yeah, Cliff, I'm beginning to think that was it."

Luke popped part of another chocolate chip bar into his mouth, "Mmmmmm."

"Maybe it's time to check in with your grandma, maybe he told her stories of his college days."

"Don't know, she's never really shared. Luke, you and me, we need some background on Dr. Montclare, granddad, hadn't even thought about that. 'Bout all I know is that he was 18 in 1945 when he started college at the U of GA."

"Keep on researching, I can tell you two are having fun with this."

"Someday, Mom and Dad, I may be a research doctor; this'll be a good start."

"And I might just end up in research too, that's a lot of what microbiology is about, still think I want to be with the CDC."

Cassie put her notebook in her backpack and smiled to Luke's parents, "Hey, thanks for listening to our story, so fascinating, history, and athletics, all mixed up together, for a banner.   Now we gotta just go, visiting, right Luke?"

5

They headed out early with the 1:30 appointment time clearly in mind. The trip to Altanhoot took them the planned four+ hours. The map from Mrs. Sarison directed them to the university's athletic department. She would be there to meet them with the athletic director and the football coach. When Cassie and Luke arrived, two more people joined them. Mrs. Sarison introduced the teens to all of them.

The reporter from the Altanhoot Recorder asked for permission to take Luke and Cassie's picture holding the banner. A university photographer also joined in with his request.

"Of course," Cassie smiled to them.

They all walked out to the football field where the photographer took shots, and the reporter kept asking questions while Cassie and Luke held the top of the banner.

"Oh, my gosh," Cassie whispered to Luke after the first picture was taken, "I never expected all this."

"Me neither," Luke shook his head, "uh, I think it's kinda a big deal for them."

"Yeah, seems to be."

"Let's head on back. I'll share with you what Sam and I want to do with the banner."

Don, the athletic director smiled to Luke and Cassie and indicated the university photographer and the city report should follow along.

"Except for photos and some athletic statistics from the university library archives we've never gotten a foothold on the athletic programs from the early days of this school. A fire before WWII took most of the history available about sports here. This is a superior huge find for us, thanks to your persistent search and the help of Mrs. Sarison."

He nodded to her and smiled to them.

"As I said earlier, I'll show you what Sam and I've thought about, with checking in with the university president who's an avid all-sports fan."

He walked with all of them to the 10-year-old field house, where athletic teams wrestled, played basketball and volleyball. He strode up and down the huge hallway with two entrances into the field house arena.

"Look at all the space available along these walls."

"We're thinking," Coach Ewing spoke up, "and already have planned for this particular wall space," he pointed along the wall, left to right and up and down, "for a metal case enclosed with glass that several student built. It'll house the banner before and after we display it out on the football field. That's for our home games. I kinda got this vision that the banner got displayed somehow back in the 20's, like someone running across the football field with it. The football announcer'll tell the story of how it got returned to us, that now we're Harriers for mascot, a change of mascot from the old days."

"Yeah, I concur with coach. That's what we're planning on doing, before our home football games. As coach suggests the announcer talks about the banner. Then we'll display it with maybe a cheerleader running, holding the banner, running across the field."

"Wow, the covered case will keep the banner material from completely disintegrating."

"That's right, Cassie, I imagine we'll only be able to do this for four or five years, then it'll be kept in this case," the athletic director pointed to the location of the case, "oh, and there'll be a plaque next to the case explaining the history of banner, how it was found again."

Coach spoke up, "The two students finished the case, and with the help of our building/ground crew we'll have it up before the first game."

Luke nodded to them all, "It's outa sight that you place significance on the banner."

Don smiled to him, "We've got a big hole in our history at the University of Triberiar. We're very grateful to you two, Cassie, especially on your follow through on your granddad's request."

After they drove away from the university Mrs. Sarison suggested a couple of places for them to see in the area around Altanhoot. They met her at her home at 5:30 p.m. A lively dinner began. Her husband, Bobby D. fixed wonderfully flavored barbequed beef, corn on the cob, salad, rolls, and fresh strawberry shortcake smothered with whipped cream. Luke and Cassie ate and ate.

"Shaw, don't think you eat quite as much as our young'uns did growin' up."

"It's so good Bobby D., where'd you learn how to fix the beef like that?" Luke asked.

"Old time, trade secret, that's all I'm gonna say," he folded his arms across his chest.

Both Luke and Cassie noted his crooked smile. The teens learned that their sons were grown and gone, both college graduates with girlfriends, but with no plans to marry.

"The wife, she'll have to wait for those grandkids," he smiled to Mary Sarison.

"In due time," she nodded to them all.

After dinner they played poker, with just chips, until Luke and Cassie felt weary.

Cassie awoke early and got into her outfit for returning home. Luke asked her to knock on his door when she got up. She decided to let him sleep. Now she tapped on the door.

"I'm getting up, thanks, Cassie."

She walked down the steps to find Bobby D. making coffee and cooking up bacon at the kitchen stove.

"Gotta send you back with a good breakfast."

By the time they finished breakfast Mary Sarison left for work. They hugged her and thanked her for her hospitality and the fine meals.

Bobby D. walked them out to Luke's dad's car and saw them off.

"Ya'll come back and visit us. We've a fine school here; not sure where you two are headed for university."

"Thank you for everything; you're a great cook," Cassie smiled up to him as she gave him a hug.

Luke and Bobby D. shook hands.

They waved to him as he stood in the driveway watching them go.

"A great dad," Cassie looked over to Luke and smiled.

"He'll make a mighty fine grandfather, I bet."

On the trip back Cassie talked about thank you notes to Mary and to Don and the coach.

"I'll do them, Luke; you're deep into cross country practice. And GMag needs me this week at the clinic. Miriam asked to take a week's vacation, so I'll hold down the front desk and help as I can."

"I've decided where I'm going to apply."

"Tell me."

"I'd save mom and dad a ton of money, if I used my HOPE scholarship and stayed in state, but I'm really not liking the idea of the UGA. And Georgia Tech, it's more for engineering and subjects like that, not so much medical."

"So those don't sound like good choices for you?"

"Nah, there's also UNC, that's part of the research triangle, but, truth, it's not that much cheaper than Notre Dame 'cause I'm out of state. And I think I got an honest shot at a scholarship, maybe academic, or sports, 'cause I'm soccer and cross country."

"What are you telling me, Luke?"

"I'll apply to all four, and see what happens. Oh, did I tell you what I'm doing on Wednesday afternoon after school? There's no cross country practice."

"Nope," she looked over to him. "We've got an hour to home. So tell me, you're pretty jammed packed right now, just a reminder, about taking a minute for yourself."

"Uh huh, I gotta do this thing."

"Do what?"

"My goal is medicine. I gotta find out what that's like. So I'm a volunteer at Ephrine Memorial."

"Really, what will that mean?"

"Uh, not sure exactly, but given that I like kids, I've asked to be placed in Pediatrics, to help out with afternoon care, time spent reading to little ones, and most important helping with the dinner hour. The volunteer coordinator tells me I'll help feed the little tots, then clean up, stuff like that, early prep for bedtime."

Cassie patted him on his right shoulder and gave him her wide smile.

"That sounds, oh wow, totally outa sight, it's where you're headed, Luke. And I'll bet whatever school you go to, you'll keep it up, some connection to young people. Pediatric oncology, I can see you doing that as a doctor."

"Long road ahead, if it's God's will, Cassie," he nodded to her.

Luke walked her up to her front door and held her bag as she unlocked it. He followed her into the spacious great room. He set down her bag. They turned to each other and hugged. Cassie lifted her face up to his. He kissed her, a soft and gentle kiss. She kissed him back, and they continued to kiss, deeper and deeper kisses. He teased his tongue into her mouth, and she slowly touched his tongue. She felt a grinding electric jolt that came from their tongues touching and also from her whole vaginal area.

"It's like I'm on fire, in my mouth and below," she thought as she took her mouth from his.

She looked up into his eyes, a smoldering brown now.

"Oh Cassie I want you, I love you. I know you feel my erection. My whole body aches, been aching for a long time, wanting you," he paused, "wanting you."

"I love you, Luke, that's all I can say for now. We've our whole sexual and loving lives ahead of us. I'm not gonna be who you'll love and cherish, down the road, years from now. So much time, I'm just glad I'm able to get to know the deep down you, your dreams, yeah and your hopes, for right now." She nodded to him, "We have to say good bye for now; you understand?"

He shook his head to her, "Sadly I do, totally I'm twitterpaited with you, do you get it?"

She nodded, "See ya, Luke, it's really important that you've been a part of my life."

Cassie walked into the kitchen, a swirl of feelings reeling through her head.

"Coffee, I need coffee, I gotta sort stuff out, my goodness, my sexual feeling for Luke, they're so powerful, I guess it's been the time we've been together, the closeness of going to the university. We've accomplished something important together, something that's significant to a university's unknown past," she spoke out.

"I just gotta find out the rest of the puzzle, if it's possible."

She drank one cup of coffee and took the second cup to her room as she sorted through her bag.

"Three days of chores to catch up on, my running , I gotta get back to that," she blew out a big breath.

∳

Cassie dug in; her junior year classes kept her up most nights until after midnight. Her a cappella group planned to enter a competition during the Halloween season.

Their singing leader let them know, "Groups swing and sway now, in addition to singing the songs. I've been noticing that for several years. There's no more standing still; now you're expected to use your arms and legs plus your voice."

With a little experimentation the Hillyer group caught on to the new way of presentation. The Ephrine High a cappella group met with the Hillyer students at the community center one afternoon after school in early October. Ephrine also planned to attend the same competition as Hillyer.

"I like what we're doing, and I like how the other school's willing to share with us," Cassie mentioned about half way through the meeting with Ephrine. She paired with a teen from Ephrine High. The two schools presented what they each were doing with their particular movements and the singing.

"We don't really wanta stop," the singers from both schools spoke up.

"But we have parents waiting, gotta break now."

The students shook hands and spoke of all the new ideas they gathered for future practices back at their own schools.

"This was a success," Cassie mentioned to a number of the singers as they made their way to the folks waiting for them.

Her music teacher caught up with her on the way to their cars.

"Cassie, thanks for being so positive, it helped our group, but it also gave the Ephrine students a chance to see what a kind a newcomer-to-the-game school, ours, has to offer. We collaborated, and you kinda took the lead for our singers."

"I've always sorta been that kind of person, see what can change, and try to help implement the change. I'll continue to help out, Mr. Hendred."

"Hey, I appreciate that; we all got big loads of stuff on our plates."

"Right on," Cassie smiled to him as she got close to her pickup.

And from that time until the holidays, Cassie's spirits continued to be lifted by all her activities.

℥

"Can't you see it, Cassie?" her friend, Kendra, pointed out as they got ready to leave the lunch room.

"See what?"

"Ian and Ethan, they like us, like to be with us, Ian, you and Ethan, me."

"'Cause we eat lunch together?"

"Yeah, there's that, every day, but sometimes they meet us after late a cappella practice.

"Uh, huh, I guess that's right."

"Has Ian asked you yet?"

Cassie shook her head to Kendra, "To what?"

"I know Evan's gonna ask me to the Holiday Ball, and I'm pretty sure he'll want to double date with Ian. Those two guys, both cross-country guys, are together a lot."

"Yeah, they are, we'll see, OK, yeah, I'd love to dance with Ian," she nodded to Kendra as they headed down the hall to their classes.

℥

"Ian's already asked me, Luke, that's why I haven't said anything to you," Cassie indicated as she looked across to him as he drove her home. They came from church after mass and the CYO meeting before that.

"Hey, here's the article back to you about the banner. The reporter in Altanhoot did a nice job, good picture of us." He handed the paper to Cassie. "Zooks, I'm disappointed, Cassie, thought you'd ask me again this year, uh, to come with you to the Holiday Ball."

"I'm doing what I want you to do, Luke, please, see other girls, like me with Ian. What we feel for each other, the love, it's important. But I love others, too, just like you do. One of the things Annie mentioned to me as she got sicker was to make sure I let love into my life, lots of love, different kinds of love, from different people."

"Keep coming with me to CYO?"

"Nah, I'll drive myself from now on, but I'll see you there. Hey," she paused, "gosh, you'll be gone away to school before we know it. I'll still come because I like our group and then there's mass after, we can sit together then, if you like. All that's important to me, my religion, attending services."

"You like your independence, being able to maneuver yourself around?"

"I do, very much."

"Growing up, we're both growing up."

"Young adults, Luke, we are," she looked to him and nodded.

ಬಿ

"You're sure, Cassie?"

"I am."

Ian and Cassie flew across the dance floor in a fast waltz.

"It's always bothered me, the way I talked to you the first time I met you. You're just so absolutely beautiful, in my eyes."

"You're forgiven, Ian, you are my friend now. I make tons of mistakes. You're learning, I guess, the hard way, how to talk to girls."

"I am, I won't forget that slap, I totally deserved it."

They stopped dancing and took a break at the table they shared with Kendra, Evan, and two younger girl dancers who didn't have a place to sit down.

"Seems like lots more little people came to the dance this year," Evan commented to the two girls.

Alicia responded for them both, "Uh huh, it's 'cause our PE teacher decided that all the grades should have a chance to learn to dance, so we all could attend the ball."

"And feel comfortable, right?" Cassie asked.

The girls responded, "Right."

Cassie almost cried as Evan and Ian danced with the fourth graders. They all were having fun with the swing dance.

"It's been a good year so far, my boards taken, making final decisions about where I want to apply to college. And having a good friend, like Ian, who was there for Annie, and now for me, every day," the thought swirled about in Cassie's head as she watched the two tall boys bring the two small girls back to the table.

Mattie and Alicia sat down, and smiled and smiled to the seniors.

"That was sssooo much fun," Mattie chirped out in her high voice.

Evan and Ian nodded as Cassie and Kendra clapped for the four of them. The rest of the evening Ian and Cassie danced, close for the slow dances, and fast for the swing. She felt the strength in his arms as she melted into his slow-dance embrace.

ℛ

"Wanta get together on New Year's Eve?"

"I'd like that, Cassie, I'm missing my sister a lot, have all this holiday season. But I've also missed you."

So they all sat together at the dining room table, having soup and sandwiches, Maggie, Cassie, Luke, and Emma. The bright fire in the fireplace and the lit Christmas tree helped Cassie feel uplifted again, knowing her loved ones were with her, there at the table and memories of loved ones in her heart.

Just as the meal concluded her grandma got a call. An emergency required her to meet Brad at the clinic. Emma left to get ready to go to a party with her parents.

Luke and Cassie sat on the couch, sipping the hot chocolate Cassie just fixed for them.

"Annie's here."

Cassie turned to Luke, "I know, she's in my heart, her memory."

"I'm obsessing about her, Cassie, I'm beginning to think I'm sick," he paused, "in the head."

"Go back and talk to Reverend Sjarlendone."

"Yeah, I need to, I gotta let her go. Her room's all fixed up at home for a guest, but when I go in there what I see is her, and I see the room as it was."

They set their cups down on the coffee table in front of them.

"I miss her."

"And I miss her," Cassie answered back as they hugged. Their tears mingled as they kissed each other, kiss after kiss.

"A new year coming, soon, a year of promise, for both of us."

They eased down, so they lay next to each other on the long couch, Luke facing Cassie. They continued their embracing. Luke moved Cassie's hand down to hold his throbbing penis. He reached up her sweater and freed one of her breasts. He caressed her nipple with his thumb and finger.

"Can't do this, can't," her mind shot back from their passion, the burning in her whole groin, to reality.

"Luke, stop, no, I'm saying no, I can't do this, with you, or to you, or with me, stop."

Cassie felt her face, wet with her tears and Luke's. Her nose sopped with liquid.

"Let me up."

Silence eased between them. He swung around and put his legs down in front of him.

"You have to go."

"I know."

"Get your coat and leave."

He stood and looked down to her, their eyes blazing into each other's, filled with tears, and wanting.

"I will always love you."

Cassie nodded to him. She lay there and talked to God. After a time she fixed her sweater, stood and shut off the gas fireplace and unplugged the Christmas tree.

"Hope, there's hope," she paused, "God?"

∞

Luke cried so hard he had to pull over on a side street aways from his home. He tried to calm himself by taking deep breaths in and out. It wasn't working. He shut his car off, pocketed his keys and got out. He ran and ran and ran. He turned around and tried to retrace his steps. Luke got lost. Two hours later he finally found his car. In the background he heard fireworks.

"It must be 1994, what a year it's gonna be," he smiled as he spoke up to the stars. He got in his car and headed home. His mom hollered to him after he took his shoes off at the front door.

"I was out running, Mom and Dad, after I left Cassie's."

"Happy New Year," he heard his dad say as he ran up the stairs to bed.

Before he drifted to sleep he resolved, "Annie's really gone, Cassie's gone, but they're still with me, in my memory, in my heart. I have that, yes, I have that."

∞

"Cassie, we're gonna have company over this weekend."

They stood in the kitchen fixing spaghetti for dinner. Maggie made the salad and Cassie cut up the French bread and slathered each piece with soft butter and garlic powder.

"Oh, yeah, glad we've done Valentine's Day, so tell me."

"Talkin' about your granddad's murky past, I got a phone call at the office. It turned out to be a fraternity brother who wanted to look Steph up. He's coming to visit, seems he and Steph got together soon after your granddad took on the veterinary practice here in Ephrine, way back in the day, before me. Then these two lost touch. The man plans to retire soon and is checking out areas of the US. He liked it here, from what he can remember back then. I cried as I had to tell him about Steph's death. The man didn't know. He cried too, what a mess, both of us bawling over the phone.

Anyhow, Blake Fosterman will visit us, and I've asked him to spend the night Saturday and Sunday. He's got stories to tell us about their days together, stuff Steph never shared with me."

"Was this before vet school, GMag?"

"Right, the University of Georgia, that's where they were fraters. I guess that's what the guys in that fraternity called each other, at least at UGA."

Cassie arrived home late that Saturday afternoon. She studied at the city library after dance class. She also looked up information about her writing project in her AP History class. She chose Eleanor Roosevelt as her subject.

"Unbelievable how much information there is on this remarkable woman," she thought as she carried her heavy backpack into the house. She brought home three books to further her Eleanor research.

"Cassie, come met Blake," she heard from the kitchen.

After he stood to greet her, Cassie shook hands with him.

"My goodness," she looked up and up, "I hope you played some hoops for UGA."

"Right on, little lady, two years, just made the varsity squad and then messed up my knee." He shook his head, "And back then, after the war, knee surgeries, well, I didn't have anything done until much later."

After a late dinner, the three of them sat around the fire in the great room.

"I'll share a little more, then I'm off to bed. Sounds like we're going hiking tomorrow, after church. Is that right, Maggie?"

She nodded to him, "Got the trail all planned out."

"Wanted to share this newspaper clipping with you, Blake, in the hope that you might be able to help me with the rest of the story about a banner."

Cassie handed the clipping to him. She watched as he read through the information in silence, then going through it again, reading out loud certain parts.

Blake shook his head, first to Cassie and then to her grandma.

"That old son of a gun, he kept the banner. I take it he never told the story, Maggie, to you?"

"Heck, I knew nothing about the banner until Cassie came to live with me, in August of 1992. He and our son, Jeff, had a conversation about returning the banner to its owner. But Steph never shared with Jeff how it all came about."

"Or who the banner belonged to," Cassie added.

"I'm impressed, the article talks about how hard you worked to find the owner, Cassie."

He smiled to her, nodding.

"Blake, I'm dying, tell us, oh please, I got my notepad to write the important stuff down."

He put his head in his hands for a moment. As he raised up he looked at Maggie and then at Cassie.

Cassie saw the twinkle in his eyes.

"The fall of 1945, the war over that August, a time of hope and future peace for our country. Steph and I, both 18, just graduated from high school. We started at the U of Georgia, us and a bunch of veterans, just home from the war, who wanted better, a college education. We were stupid, spoiled kids who knew the war from listening to the radio and reading the newspapers."

He stopped, "Not like now, everything's becoming instantaneous. Well, we had no concept, had a lot to learn from the vets. So our fraternity, which we pledged spring of our freshman year, had us young guys, and a little bit older, more mature men, who'd fought and seen others die, for our country. It was so good to have them in our midst. The older guys kept us from doing really stupid stuff."

"Did you and granddad know each other before the fraternity?"

"No, the fraternity really was our college family. The next fall our group decided we would meet up with our fraternity brothers at Georgia Tech, and we had a chapter at the University of Triberiar. We met the fraters there."

Cassie smiled, "Uh huh this is starting to make some sense," she thought.

"Part of our house visited Atlanta, for Tech. Steph and I and other fraters headed for Triberiar. We took along our fall pledge class, half to Tech and half with us to Triberiar. The pledges had a task."

Cassie started to laugh," Oh man, what did you guys have them do?"

Blake looked at her and smiled, "It turned out so cool. The pledges were on a scavenger hunt in the house, as all of us actives got entertained by the fraters there, same deal at Tech in Atlanta."

Maggie nodded her head, "The pledges took certain items, all to be returned, right?"

"Uh huh, that was the plan. Unfortunately, a couple of items never made it back. The way Steph tells it, his little brother gave him the banner. Finding a banner was on that pledge's list. He found it in one fraternity brother's room at the frat house at the U of T. But somehow, between Steph and his little brother, neither made sure it got returned to the house. I got my little brother's item back to the fraternity house."

"So Steph forgot, or didn't want to share what the story was behind the banner?" Maggie asked.

"Looks that way, life got lived and time got away from your husband, Maggie. And then from what you've shared, he got sick, and sicker. There was too much for him to deal with, so."

Cassie added, "He passed it on to my dad. He must have understood the importance of the banner, keeping it all those years."

"Yeah, Cassie, he was pretty conscientious about that sort of thing. I just wished he'd shared," Maggie added.

"Or maybe because the banner said hawks, and he knew the school's mascot was harriers, all confusing."

"Well, maybe your granddad felt embarrassed about not dealing with it, and then," Blake paused, "as I said before he knew time and life were getting away from him, he asked for help. There was a lot he had to deal with, the future for Maggie, taking care of the clinic, the business he had for so many years he wanted it to go on, I'm sure."

"Yeah, GMag and Blake, he finally asked for help."

Cassie stopped talking and then started to tear up, "I had a friend, a girl my age, who was dying of cancer, over a year ago. She asked for help, to put in place all the things she wanted her folks and brother to do, with her and for her, before she died, and stuff afterward. She asked for time with her friends, planned her own celebration of life. And, she wanted to help with cancer research, so she donated her own body to further the cause."

"What was her name, Cassie?"

"Annie."

Blake looked directly at her, "You know what?"

"What's that?"

"You, young lady, were lucky to have Annie in your life, an example of how to be brave, strong, in the face of death."

"Yeah, God stayed next to her, during that whole time and now in heaven. Annie talked about God a lot, about being so happy to be going to Him."

The great room remained silent as each of them took time to contemplate.

"I am so glad you shared your story, Blake. I just need a couple of pieces of information, and if it's OK, I want to let the University of Triberiar know about how the banner got to be in the hands of my granddad."

"Have to tell you ladies," he laughed and smiled to them, "it was such a fun outing, that weekend so many years ago, time spent in Triberiar, getting to know other men who shared our values and plans for our futures."

"Sounds like it was a hopeful time for our country, Blake."

"It was, don't you think so, Maggie?"

"Yes, our countrymen back with us, so many plans, college, women began to want careers, too."

"Like you, right Grandma?"

"Like me."

"So I don't know your background, Maggie Montclare, school?"

"Right, Berkeley, uh, the U. of California, Berkeley, for my undergrad."

"Vet school?"

"Lucky for me, being a California kid, I got into U. of California, Davis Vet School."

"How'd you end up in Georgia?"

"Start of my senior year, read granddad's ad," Maggie smiled to Cassie, "in a vet digest. I visited that Christmas. Steph wanted an assistant to eventually partner with him. I'd never been to the South. And, well, I graduated and came to the Montclare Clinic in Ephrine. A few months later we married, and then your dad joined us."

The three of them attended early mass. Blake took them out to brunch at the homey restaurant Maggie and Cassie loved.

"Want to come with us on our hike?"

"Nah, GMag, I got a super ton of homework, the Eleanor paper to finish researching and write, and the first thing I'll do is write my letter to Mrs. Sarison at the University of Triberiar. I know she'll get the story to the football coach and athletic director. I'd like to write my letter by hand on the nice stationery I used for my letters of inquiry. Do you think that's OK?"

"Yes."

Maggie went on to share with Blake about how Cassie and Luke got to know the folks at the University of Triberiar.

"Think you might want to go there, Cassie?" Blake asked.

"Nope, I'm going for microbiology, got a couple of schools picked out."

"She knows her own mind, Maggie."

"Yes she does, she's my granddaughter," Maggie touched Cassie's shoulder and smiled to them both.

℘

Cassie stood on the hillside near the park at the west edge of Ephrine. Ian told her where she could see the cross country teams run, during the competition on that Saturday in April. She got out of dance practice and realized that she still could make the approximate time the teams would run. She saw the guys running, Hillyer in their red shirts and four other teams. She couldn't remember for sure the Ephrine High school colors. She peered closer. Ian and Luke ran neck and neck along the trail assigned for the meet.

"It's gonna be close. The results will be in the paper tomorrow."

When she drove into the garage, she made up her mind.

"This's been driving me crazy since New Year's Eve. I'm gonna tell grandma. I miss Luke, but Ian and I are good friends."

Cassie cooked dinner of oven-baked pork chops, corn, salad, rolls, and cheese cake for dessert. Maggie got home earlier and took a nap. Cassie noticed how much tireder her grandma look at the end of a workday. It had something to do with the stable fire. She also let go of her Wednesday afternoon appointments, giving Brad those appointments. Maggie often went on a hike away from Ephrine on that afternoon.

After dinner cleanup they took their dessert to the couch in front of the fire place, lit on this cool spring eve.

"Grandma, I need to share."

They each took a bite of their cheese cake and set their plates down on the table along with their coffee. Maggie took Cassie's hand as she watched tears sparkle in her eyes.

"Go ahead, tell me."

"New Year's Eve, you had an emergency at the clinic and Emma left to go to a party with her parents. Luke and I sat right here, next to each other. We began talking about Annie, about missing her, about our love for her. That's how it started, then our kissing and caressing. But pretty soon after that things spiraled."

"Uh huh, outa control, he stopped when you asked him to?"

Cassie looked directly into her grandma's blue eyes, "Yes, he did. And I love him for that. GMag, I had no idea how fast passion could pull a person into wanting to be one, to couple with someone you love. I thought I was strong. But, that instinct, that wanting to connect with another, that's the most powerful feeling I've ever encountered. I have my self-respect, and I know Luke has his. But it coulda been a whole different situation."

"Lesson learned?"

"Oh yeah, but it's brought me so much pain, regret and I couldn't even talk about it until now."

"Happened to me, Cassie."

"No way, Grandma?"

"Yes way, except for me alcohol and a big group of people all mingling together was how it happened, a second date. Not like for you, in the quiet, with someone you really cared about."

"Did you like the guy?"

"I did, but I'd only met him on a date for a football game a few weeks before. We had a great time, the game, the food and party after."

"What did you have to do?"

"Stupid shit, I was," she shook her head, "the alcohol screwed my judgement. When he wouldn't stop, I said no. He still wouldn't. And he was super juiced up, on grain alcohol and grape juice, no less."

"That stuff'll make you blind."

"Uh huh, I slugged him in the eye. I aimed too high, cripes it sorta knocked him out. That ended that. He could'a been a nice friend, but that was the end."

"Yeah, for me and Luke, too."

"You see him at CYO?"

"Right, but we sit apart at mass, now."

"Cassie, there are wonderful men out there, like your granddad and your dad, and you'll meet a lot of them in college. Don't judge by this one situation."

"I won't; I got a question though, now that Blake's filled us in about the banner, the situation there, I'd like to let Luke know what I'm doing, the letter to Mrs. Sarison."

"My suggestion?"

"Sure could use it."

"I'll make several copies of the letter and then mail the original with your envelope to Mrs. Sarison."

"So then I could mail Luke a copy of the letter. He'll know the complete banner story."

Maggie smiled to her granddaughter and thought, "My oh my, she's growing up, finding tough parts of life, like I did, for which she'll always have to deal. But she can handle it, yes she can."

&

Cassie wrote her letter to Mrs. Sarison, sharing the banner story pretty much the way Blake explained it to her and her grandma. And she got a handwritten note, from Luke. He handed it to her as she left CYO on a Sunday in May. She put it in her purse and forgot to retrieve it until she put her purse away the next day.

"Definitely I'm going to this," she told Maggie about Luke's invitation to an after-graduation party. "Grandma, you're on the invitation too."

"I'd very much like to come, but it'll have to be in my clinic clothes. You go earlier, after dance class. I've not seen Luke since New Year's Eve."

"He's going to Notre Dame."

"That was his first choice, right?"

"It was, possibility he'll get a little money help, depends on how soccer works out for him there."

"Think he can handle the work load, and sports?"

"Can't say, Grandma."

ℂ

Cassie came up the walk to the Ingraham front door. She watched balloons tied to the front porch columns wave in the light breeze. Her breath caught in her throat.

"Oh, Annie, I'm sure you see all this, the celebration and joy of a high school graduation party, you're here, my dear, with me, and Luke and your folks."

She rang the doorbell. Luke greeted her with a smile and hug.

"Thank you for coming, Cassie."

"Maggie'll be here when she gets away from the clinic later."

"Great!"

Cassie heard the music in the background. Luke definitely was a throwback to the 60"s as she heard the sounds throughout the first floor of the Ingraham home. She found Luke's parents and thanked them for including her and her grandma in the celebration. She ate a plate of fried chicken, beans, potato salad, and drank a pop. She felt someone come to the side of her.

"Cassie, you're here," she recognized his deep voice before she turned.

"Ian, I didn't know you'd be here."

"Glad I am, you know, the four of us, we had some sad, and then some glad times together after Annie. By the way, I feel her here."

He sat next to her on a ledge in the back yard. He had a plate filled with food.

He watched her nod, "Yeah, for reals, Annie's here, she wouldn't miss this celebration, she and Luke, wow, their love for each other, it was somethin'."

"It was, I hurt so bad for him, the way he cried in our first couple meetings with my dad."

"He's better, movin' on with his life. Emma told me she saw him a little bit, uh, an actual date. The best, he's going away to school. He needs that, new people in his life."

"We're friends now Ian, me and you, so I'll tell you that Luke and I haven't dated since last year. We had to let each other go."

"For the best, right?"

"Exactly."

"We got lots of decisions to make, our futures. What about you and this summer?"

"Working at the clinic, and one noon a week, I help with the food at our homeless shelter."

"It's awful, Cassie, how many folks are in need of help. You know how blessed we are?"

"Beyond belief, I do. Oh Emma's invited me to come with her to visit her grandparents in Atlanta next week."

"Yeah, it'll be good for you to get away. Your grandma stays so busy; you two don't get much time together."

"We go on hikes on afternoons off, and talk at dinner together. I always have studying."

"So this summer will be a good break for you. I want to do stuff with you, Cassie. I'm working maintenance at the city golf course; it's horrible grunt work in our jinormous sun and heat. Makes me appreciate AC and evenings."

They laughed together.

"Let's get more, I need another plate."

"Ian, I'm headed to the dessert area."

Out of the corner of her eye she saw Emma and Luke talking together.

"I'm so happy to see them smiling, caring for each other. Thank you, God, for that answered prayer. I been praying that they might like each other and spend time together before Luke leaves," Cassie thought.

"You're far away," Ian stood next to her getting cake.

"Just thinkin,' I'm happy for the folks here, for us. The Ingraham home, you could, honest, cut the pain with a knife, before Annie left them."

They returned to the seats on the outside ledge.

"You decided, about school?"

"Yeah, Mrs. Brooks and I talked just this last week. I qualify for the HOPE scholarship, so I'll seek admission to the University of Georgia."

He turned to her, "Yeah, I can hear the wheels in your brain turning. Mrs. Brooks emphasized it so much to me. If, if I get the HOPE, I know I have to make good grades every single semester. If my GPA falls below the HOPE standard, it's all over."

Cassie touched his shoulder, "You'll not let that happen 'cause you know you gotta keep the scholarship."

"Thanks for your confidence; we'll all be hopin' for the best. I'll work hard and it'll be a fine school for me, think accounting, I love math. Cassie, I gotta have financial help. My folks can't do it alone, with the ministry and mom just working part time so she can help at church without having to pay an extra helper."

"Uh huh, I know you live frugal-like."

"We have to, in order to make it every month. I was so lucky when my uncle just handed over the pickup to me. He musta known, it's tough at our house. I gotta keep working to keep up the insurance and plates, and college."

They each got lost in their thoughts for a moment.

"You still planning on University of Wisconsin?"

"Yeah, the Madison campus, it's the school with the microbiology program I'm looking for."

"You'll need a new wardrobe, and what about your old pickup?"

"Coat, boots, hat, gloves, remember we sometimes need that stuff here."

"More heavy duty there."

"Yeah, and I'm not taking wheels. We hardly ever seen snow, let alone drive around in the cold stuff."

They laughed together, holding their arms out, pretending to maneuver around in the ice and snow

&CapitalE;

"It's been so much fun, so relaxing, spending time with Emma, you and Grandpa Ernest."

Cassie hugged Emma's grandma as the three women sat together in a restaurant in a downtown mall in Atlanta.

"We've seen a play, a concert, and both Cassie and I enjoyed church on Sunday."

"Fabulous singers, at your church, they really know how to glorify God."

"Emma told us that you sing in your school's a cappella group. So we understand your appreciation for our singers. They don't need anything but their own voices."

"Grandma Sally, truth is, those men and women've got a truly divine gift."

Emma added, "I told you, Cassie."

The two teens discussed the musical ability of the grandparents' church members even before they attended a Sunday service. And that evening, their last one in Atlanta before Emma's folks came to pick them up, the teens wanted to cook a dinner for Emma's grandparents. Grandma Sally and the girls shopped for the groceries the girls needed along with grandma's other grocery list.

Emma deferred to Cassie about the cooking of the meal. Together they had fun sharing the responsibilities, Cassie giving orders and Emma following through. The pork chops baked up just right, with easy cutting of the tender and juicy meat. Dessert turned out to be a surprise; the grandparents enjoyed the cheesecake and mixed berries immensely.

"Delicious, dessert delicious, the whole meal, young ladies, was outstanding," Grandpa Ernest smiled and nodded to them as the girls took away the dessert plates and cleaned up after the meal.

"Cassie, before you leave us, we know you have concerns for Emma."

They sat in the family room, grandpa sipping his cognac, and the ladies having their decaf coffee.

"Confession, when I first met your folks, Emma, at Annie's celebration." Cassie paused, "Emma's told you about our friend, Annie, who lost her fight with cancer."

Grandpa Ernest nodded, "We kept Annie in our prayers, still do."

Cassie began again, "Well, I told myself, a nice black couple, obviously, adopting a white girl. Then I checked in with my grandma. And Emma, I got a shocker, when grandma, she told me the folks you introduced me to, they were your biological parents. We've never talked about it."

Emma nodded to Cassie, "No, we've never."

Grandma Sally sat between the teens on a bright red couch. She picked up pictures from the table in front of them.

"Emma, not sure how long it's been since you've seen these."

Sally pointed out the blonde woman in the beautiful white gown.

"Girls, this is my mother, Sara Ann."

"A stunning young lady, wow, from back in the day."

"She was, and she was the love of my dad's life."

Grandma Sally handed the next picture to Cassie.

"He's my dad, Andrew."

Cassie gave the picture to Emma, "So handsome, I can see how they'd have been attracted."

Finally Grandma Sally held their wedding picture. And she shared with Cassie and Emma their love story.

"Thank you Grandma, my mom, she always told me to ask you about your folks."

"And I have shared, my dears, it's a wonderful story, and I am very proud of my parents, how they stood by each other in the face of very difficult circumstances. And they died, within a few days of each other, at just about the time I graduated from college.   They wanted that more than anything, for their daughter to have a degree and an immediate profession."

"So Grandma Sally, what was your life's work before retirement?"

"Teacher and school administrator."

"Same for me," Grandpa Ernest spoke up.   "But we also got extremely lucky in the stock market.   That was fun, an extra challenge for us as we got older."

"Your mom and dad shared with us that you struggled for a time with who you were, Emma.   And it seems that you are starting to make decisions, is that correct?"

"Right, and I am glad Cassie is here with me.   We've been through a lot together."

"That's for certain," Cassie added.

"I discussed this with my counselor at Ephrine.   She understands what I've decided to do on my applications to UGA and Tech, uh, and mom and dad know."

"Tell us."

"I am black, and that's how I'll fill out my application."

Grandpa Ernest interjected, "Absolutely your decision, my granddaughter."

Emma looked around, and gave eye contact to each of them.

"I'm not doing it to please anyone.   I know, in my heart, who I am.   Annie became my impetus, the way she made decisions about the end of her life."

"Me and Emma," then she heard what she just said, "sorry I shouldn't blow it in front of teachers."

She heard laughter from the grandparents.

"Emma and I," Cassie paused, "heard Annie telling us about how much wonderful life we had yet to live, so many more years than she would have."

At that both Emma and Cassie teared and grabbed hands across Grandma Sally. She put an arm around each teen and held them close.

℘

Emma's folks drove to Cassie's home. They saw four cars parked, two in the driveway and two out front.

"GMag must be having a picnic for the clinic; it's after work on Saturday, those are employees' cars. Thank you for driving us, Sam and Denise."

Denise looked back and nodded to Cassie

"It was our pleasure."

"Cassie, I'm so lucky to have my grandparents in my life; I've visited every year since forever."

"Emma could because teachers have a little bit more time during the summer."

Emma walked Cassie up to her door, carrying the package she had for her grandma. Cassie let herself in. The teens hugged.

"It was the best, thank you, Emma."

Cassie stood in the doorway and waved to the family after Emma got in the car.

She heard voices coming from the great room. She peeked in and saw them, Brad, GMag, Kay Ann, and Analease.

6

"Come join us, Cassie, after you get a chance to unwind from your travels."

After she put her suitcase and package in her room, she headed down and stopped at the kitchen. She didn't see preparations for a picnic.

"There's lemonade and your unfrozen chocolate chip bars in here," she heard Kay Ann say.

She took a napkin and grabbed a bar. Someone handed her a glass of lemonade. Cassie plunked down on the floor near her grandma. She smiled to the group and noticed that everyone had pen and paper in hand.

"Your trip?" Brad asked.

"Super wonderful," she nodded to him.

When she smiled to everyone, they did not smile back, not even her grandma. Cassie felt her stomach cramp; she tried to choke down a swallow of lemonade. A cold sweat started on her forehead.

"I'll speak for the clinic; your grandma's not feeling well, not wanting to talk much so we'll share with you."

Kay Ann went on, "For awhile, Maggie hasn't felt well."

She saw the questioning in Cassie's wide eyes.

"I know, I know, she didn't say anything to us either. She had tests done. So while you were in Atlanta, she had more tests.   On Monday she'll be in Macon for an aortic valve replacement. Your grandma's heart suffers."

Maggie reached down, Cassie raised up, and they hugged each other.

Cassie burst out, "Oh, grandma, will you be OK?"

Maggie patted Cassie's shoulder as she sat back down on the floor.

"Will be good as new, it's a procedure there're doing lots of now. I have every confidence in the surgeon."

"What's the plan, everybody, what's the plan?"

The group began to laugh.

"Oh dear God, what, what?" Cassie spoke out as she looked around, her eyes bright with concern.

"Those are the exact words Maggie said you would say."

"Yes folks, I do know my granddaughter."

Cassie turned and grabbed hands with her grandma again. They held on.

One by one the group explained what would happen.

"The clinic will operate as normal; Brad will take most of the load and may back off from some his farm and ranch visits, except for emergencies."

"I'm still needed?" Cassie asked.

Finally her grandma spoke up, "I need you, Cassie. Macon will be about four days. But that's not the real story. I've got a five to eight week recuperation."

"Oh my gosh, GMag, that means you can't work at the clinic?"

"No, I can't, not for a couple of months. I can't even drive for quite a while."

"I got it; you chauffeured me around forever; now I get to return the favor."

"Think you can handle riding around in that old pickup, Maggie?" Brad inquired. He emphasized the word old.

Cassie heard the laughter from the group.

"Hey, don't laugh, Cassie loves her old heap. She refuses to drive my wheels."

"Yeah, it's too fancy for my taste, a van," she giggled, shaking her head to her grandma.

"Someone said, take most of the load at the clinic; who's gonna handle the rest?"

"Cassie, remember the gentleman you met, who helped you with the background on the banner?"

"Yeah, GMag, Blake, granddad's frater, he was great and so helpful to me."

"Blake's helping us out at the clinic."

"Oh my gosh, is he a vet, I never did ask his profession?"

She gave her grandma a wide-eyed look of surprise.

"He is, licensed in Georgia along with a couple of other states."

"Was he at Auburn, for vet school, with granddad?"

"No, he graduated from Cornell's vet school."

"Sorry, I'll ask grandma more when we're finished, please go on, everyone."

Cassie listened as the group worked their way through the plan for the two to three months of Maggie's absence.

After the group left, Cassie insisted that her grandma go to her room and rest. Cassie cleaned up and decided to have chef salads for a light dinner. She put the eggs on to boil. Hundreds of images flashed through her mind of her mom's cancer, death, and of her freshman and sophomore years. She put her whole self into making a life for her and her dad.

"Grandma makes it sound like this is an OK deal, but."

She stopped talking as her thoughts flew, "Like I've always been, God, oh God, I'm in your hands, and it's Your will for me, for GMag, like it's always been and always'll be."

She let the eggs cool in the sink and ran upstairs to check on her grandma.

"Heard you Cassie, I'll get up, you puttering in the kitchen. So I know you've got something planned."

They sat together having their salads at the breakfast nook.

"Pretty big shock."

"Yeah, GMag it sure is. I had noticed after the fire that you, well, seemed to feel more tired by the time you got home from the clinic, in your face and the slump in your shoulders you sometimes had."

"You miss nothing, granddaughter," she smiled to Cassie.

"Fill me in about Blake."

"You'll keep asking so I'll fill in the gaps."

They moved to the great room to share the couch. Cassie brought the decaf coffee for them.

"As I said, Blake went off to Cornell to vet school. He married and had a son who chose a military career, like your dad's doing. He went through a sort of mid-life crisis. After the boy went away to college, Blake divorced his wife. He sold out his vet practice in New Hampshire and went into the Peace Corps, doing vet work in Sub-Saharan Africa. He got called back to deal with his ailing parents and decided to stay. He's been doing fill-in vet work in several locations since their deaths. So he's worked across the US, and he likes this area."

"Staying in Ephrine?"

"Yes, for now, he's rented a place and wants to settle down."

"So you know old questioning me, Grandma are you interested in him?"

"I can't answer that, since my mind's in such a swirl with my procedure on Monday. All I know is that we need help; Brad can't do it alone, and I need to keep all three women working for me. So Kay Ann will work with Blake as his assistant, Analease will continue with Brad."

"Makes sense, he can man the clinic so that Brad can continue calls out on the farms and ranches."

"Exactly, that's the plan."

"Oh my gosh, what about the drive to Macon?"

"You'll stay here; I'll not have you sit around a dumb germ-filled hospital waiting for me."

"Who's taking you?"

"Kay Ann, and she'll pick me up when I'm released."

"That's when I'll take over."

"Right, but Cassie, if you will, I'd like you to continue your Wednesday noon helping at the Homeless Shelter. It's community service, and I've never had time to do that kind of volunteer work. So you're standing in as a representative of the Montclare household. And dance, please keep it up through the summer and next school year, such great exercise and perhaps you'll do something in community theater."

"You're wrong, GMag about never doing volunteer work. I can think of a dozen different times since I've lived here where you helped out with animals, and never charged a dime to the animal owner."

Maggie paused, and nodded her head, "I guess you're right."

Cassie turned her eyes to her grandma's.

"I been through this with dad about mom. So I got some very serious questions that we must know about before you leave."

"Like what, Cassie?"

"Like, do you have a DNR (Do Not Resuscitate) designation, like mom had?"

"I do."

"Grandma, I know you're gonna make it through all this just fine, but still, I'll ask, is your will and power of attorney updated?"

"Uh huh, our attorney knows my situation. He's executor of my estate since Jeff is unavailable for awhile. Ever since your granddad died I have our home and clinic, the paperwork completely up-to-date."

Cassie felt the tears flood her face, "You know I can take this since I been through it with dad, what happens to our home and clinic?"

"It will all be sold."

"What about your staff?"

"They've been prepped; the staff and I, we all learned so much after granddad died, I kept them in the loop on everything that transpired."

"And me, Grandma?"

Maggie put her arm around Cassie's shoulder.

"I'll come out of this procedure better than ever."

"But?"

Cassie's blue eyes blazed into GMag's.

"Emma's folks will help you through your senior year. They've consented to have you come and live with Emma and them. Remember your college and graduate school money is already set aside. So you have no money worries."

"So dad knows?"

"No, he does not. That's my confidence level, I'm going to be just fine. My biggest problem when I get home will be all the free time I'll have, time to fret and stew about every little thing."

"I'll help keep you busy, every day. We'll walk, then little hikes, until you can drive, then, wow, you'll be able to go do your own thing until the doc says you're ready to go back to work."

"This's so hard, Cassie. So much emotion, in what we've just talked about, end-of-life decisions."

They hugged at the couch. Cassie took the coffee cups to the kitchen. She saw her grandma begin to go up the stairs.

"Early church, GMag, no CYO for rest of summer."

"Let's do it."

ଔ

Ian and Cassie planned a run for late Sunday morning. His church had an earlier time for the service during the summer. So they could be together before it got unbearably hot and humid.

Cassie met him at the park where they ran. All during the run Cassie talked about her grandma and the future. Ian listened. She stopped half way through the run and plopped in the grass. Ian saw the tears streaming down her face. He sat down next to her and took her in his arms.

"You're the strongest person I know, Cassie. God's got the answer. We just gotta wait for it."

Cassie felt the knife-like pain in her gut subside as she calmed down.

"Let's say a prayer for Grandma Maggie."

First Ian spoke and then Cassie added the Lord's Prayer.

Ian jumped up and gave Cassie his hand to pull her to her feet. They sipped their water and got ready for the final leg of their run. Cassie felt the humid air whip across her face as she ran along. Ian stayed with her, not running ahead as he sometimes did.

"Ian, run, don't wait on me. I'll catch up. I'm feeling better now."

He did, and it took Cassie a couple of minutes longer to finish. She watched him stand there, casual, hand on his hip.

"Better?"

"Yeah, there's nothing like exercise to pull a person up from the dumps."

"It's one of the reasons I'm out for cross country; I get depressed, and there's this high to running that's better than anything, makes me feel so alive."

"Time to go?"

"Yeah, GMag is leaving in a couple hours for Macon. So I wanta be there before she goes. I was so happy to be in church with her this morning."

"I'm glad we ran. I'm headed home to rest 'cause I'm still getting used to my work outside, it's so, it just whacks me out."

Cassie smiled to him, "But such good exercise."

They hugged.

"Thank you for running with me, Ian."

"I love being with you. I will be with you every step of the way through your grandma's recovery, and beyond that."

Cassie gazed at him for a moment, "I know," she paused, "your blue eyes, Ian, I see right into your soul."

He stood there and smiled.

℘

"Time for me to go, Cassie. I'll call you as soon as I can from the hospital after the procedure. I'll be home soon."

"I'll be strong, Grandma Maggie, I'll be strong."

"I know you will be."

They walked hand and hand to Kay Ann's car.

She turned to Cassie.

"I'm planning a trip for us, Cassie, to Madison, WI, in October. I want you to see the campus where I know you're planning to go to school. It's gorgeous back in that country, the fall colors."

They hugged. As she saw them off, she waved to her grandma, and Maggie waved back.

She strode up the walkway to the front door, head held high, and shoulders back. She whispered, "God, help me, guide me in what I'm supposed to do."

She turned around before she went in. Her eyes gazed from one side of the yard to the other. She hadn't mowed in awhile. After she had a glass of lemonade, she opened the French doors to the backyard.

"GMag's roses, oh my goodness."

Cassie picked deadheads from the rose bushes. Weeds grew where her grandma used to pull them away from the flowers.

"Where've I been; why hadn't I seen the neglect. Grandma Maggie hasn't felt well for some time. I got so wrapped up in my own life. I gotta step up."

Cassie mowed the front and back lawns. She weeded the rose bushes. By then she drenched in her own sweat, so she turned on the back hose and watered her face, arms, and legs. For a little while the cool felt better. As she dried off in the sun she began her plan for GMR, Grandma Maggie's Recuperation. She retraced her steps and looked over the yards.

"Better, now go inside, need clean sheets on the bed for my returning surgery patient."

❧

Tuesday evening Emma and Cassie went out to dinner together.

"You seem very happy, Cassie, your grandma, it's good news, right."

"Very, procedure went, as planned. She'll be home tomorrow evening. The hospital keeps them until all the docs and staff sign off. Hey, she's doing a bit of walking in the halls, and she says she's lots happier when she's up on her feet."

"Is she tiring?"

"Yeah, needs lots of rest time. That'll drive her crazy. She's always been active."

"You'll have to get her into some hobbies, where she can be off her feet."

"Yeah, she brought home a bunch of vet journals to catch up on. Plus, I've quizzed her, she's got such a science background. But she's missed reading a bunch of the classics, American and English."

"Do you think she can tolerate non-scientific reading?"

"Don't know, but I'm sure gonna find out. I've got a pile of books for her to start on. Oh, and we've promised each other to learn to cook several Mediterranean dishes together."

"Supposed to be good for the heart."

"Yeah, Maggie's heart, and mine."

❧

Luke sat next to Cassie and Maggie at early service the Sunday before he left for Notre Dame. He asked to go to church with them and to take them out to brunch after. At their favorite restaurant they ate brunch and talked about their summers.

"Are you feeling more back to your old self, Maggie?"

"I am, Luke, I know you're keen to do pediatric medicine, but my goodness, huge advances are being made in the coronary field. Don't discount that area of medicine, I'm pretty sure the procedure saved my life."

Cassie looked across to Luke.

"Spill," she paused, "we haven't seen you for awhile, so tell us."

"You two, and Emma, and Ian, well you'll sorta understand."

Cassie looked first at her GMag. She turned her eyes to him. Luke watched her questioning blue eyes.

"Mom and dad, they're splitting up, selling our home, too many memories there. There're each gonna buy smaller places."

Cassie saw pain flash across him face, his forehead furrowed, eyes squinting and the thin set of his lips.

There was silence at the table for a little while.

Maggie shook her head, "We're so sorry, Luke. Is there any way we can help?"

"Prayers, many many prayers."

"We can do that."

Cassie burst out, "You know blunt me, I'm looking at your next few years," she quieted, "the money, for your schooling?"

"Yeah, my dad, good old CPA, he made sure I'd be covered. They'd planned, since Annie and I were born, on our college funds. Annie understands where the money goes, don't you Annie?"

He looked up to the ceiling, then patted his heart.

"She does."

Luke walked them to Cassie's pickup after they left the restaurant.

"Cassie still wheelin' you around a bit?"

"She is, some days I still feel a bit weak, not wanting to drive. This was one of those days."

"Maggie, take care of yourself, lots of animals are depending on you, uh, also their owners," he nodded to her.

They hugged. Maggie went ahead and got in the passenger side.

Cassie and Luke looked into each other's eyes and read each other's minds, their love for each other, unspoken.

"Good luck and God speed, Luke."

"Have another fabulous year at Hillyer."

They hugged and stood together in that hug for a time. He kissed her on the top of her head. Cassie got in the pickup and looked straight ahead.

"God bless and keep Luke."

Luke walked at a slow stride to his sedan. He did not look back.

℘

"I'm so excited to be here, GMag."

They stood in the center of campus with students milling all about, heading to classes and labs and the student union.

"I have another surprise, Cassie."

Maggie held her hand as they walked to a tall man with his back turned. Maggie touched his shoulder, and he turned around. Cassie looked up and into his face. It took her a second.

"Oh my gosh, Dad, it's you, Dad."

Cassie raised up her arms and hugged him around his neck.

"Hey, Cassie, my sweet wonderful girl," he whispered to her.

Cassie stepped back and burst into tears.

"How?" she questioned as she shook her head to her dad and grandma.

"Serendipity, my dear," she heard her grandma's voice.

They sat together having coffee in a student union dining area.

"Tell me, Dad."

Jeff Montclare went on to explain his mom's phone call that she and Cassie were visiting UW, Madison and the dates. He happened to be back in the States. It was just a couple days until his new assignment which he couldn't talk about or tell where he'd be. He caught a military hop and rented a car to Madison.

"This is where I'll be, Dad. I want the science, the chance to work in labs, to be with other students who're asking, "What do we do now, with the difficult problems we've got in health?"

"Been admitted?"

"No Dad, the app's in process, but I have every confidence."

"One concern, Cassie, hadn't mentioned it to mom." He turned his gaze to Maggie.

"This is one monstrous campus, how many students?"

"Some 40,000."

"Gonna get lost in the shuffle of huge classes, of being unknown?"

"Not for long, Dad, I got so much AP credit It's possible I'll be a second semester freshman when I walk in the door next fall. That'll mean the start of smaller classes in the chems and biology."

"How's that?"

"Cause so many kids flunk out of first semester in chemistry and org chemistry and biology, which I've already passed out of. I've checked, UW's considering all my AP credits. I'm so lucky I'm in a high school with such strong academics. That's thanks to your efforts, GMag."

Cassie stopped.

"Oh Dad, and of course, your efforts over the years, plus Mom."

Cassie patted her heart as she teared up.

"Mom, you're here, right?"

Her dad touched Cassie's cheek, "Right here with us."

The three of them walked for several hours on campus, using a map to find their way around, to some of the buildings where Cassie would learn and study.

Maggie spoke up, "Feeling really tired, let's eat."

Jeff and Cassie laughed at the quirk in her voice as she said eat.

They found a pub for early dinner not far from the university.

"Dad, the research here, it's unbelievable, they're student positions, summer time and other stuff, for kids to get involved in research, even just after their first year. That's what I want, and I know I can do the work."

"So, when you get here, you plan to stay in this area, graduate?"

"Uh huh, do the dorm thing, don't want the mess of an apartment, or the cooking, wanta study and meet others; my time, it's so precious."

"You'll come home for the holidays?"

"Always, GMag."

"Hope you like snow, and cold."

"Yeah, Dad, it's a beautiful October day, but I know that's not the case for long. I'm a thin-blooded southerner, but I'll toughen up, like you always say 'it's not the cold that'll get ya, it's incorrect clothing.'"

"Wow, I did?"

Cassie heard surprise in his voice. They laughed together.

"We're getting her all geared up for that, Jeff."

They walked after their meal and took in the sights of the several blocks of night time activities.

"Dad, you're staying at our hotel?"

"I am, so I'll see you ladies in the morning for breakfast. Then I gotta head out."

"Us too, plane to catch early afternoon. I got clinic tomorrow, and Cassie has school."

"I missed Tuesday and today, but it was worth it to see my future."

"Priceless," Jeff hugged his daughter.

80

"I'm so happy," she spoke out.

Cassie gazed out at empty chairs in the Ephrine Civic Auditorium. She did see that some seats had visitors.

She listened for the cues from the orchestra in the pit in front of the stage. When she heard the appropriate note, she sang and danced with the other actors. The story of Conrad Birdie unfolded.

"Fun, this's been so much fun, I'm glad I had the courage to try out."

She and her group exited the stage. Cassie nodded to Emma, who just went on stage right with a group of dancers. She counted herself lucky because she had both dance and singing backgrounds; the singing from her years with Hillyer's a cappella singers. Tonight was dress rehearsal. And then Friday and Saturday night, and Sunday afternoon the folks in Ephrine could attend. Cassie would have three chances to perform, as a Sweet Apple teen in *Bye Bye Birdie*. She and the other Sweet Apple's would do solos in the songs, *The Telephone Hour* and *A Lot of Livin' to Do*.

For weeks now, on rehearsal nights, Cassie drove home to many hours of studying for the next day, the next test. But when the play ended, she would have a break from Hillyer for several days, and then the big push to her graduation.

She hugged her grandma after she arrived home from striking the set after that Sunday afternoon performance.

"Might be the last time I ever sing and dance like that, but Grandma, it's been wonderful, a joy to perform, mostly I study, and I'm glad to know there are other things I'm capable of."

"Once again, I'm pleased I pushed you to stay with dance, that glorious exercise, a hobby you can do for the rest of your life."

℁

"It's the one weekend this summer the four of us'll all be in town."

"Cassie, invite them over, have a late picnic out back; ask them to bring something, you know like we always do."

"Thanks, GMag."

"Ian, if you're free, join us Saturday evening, me, Luke, Emma, my house, a potluck, bring dessert."

"I miss you, Cassie, this'll be great, haven't seen the other guys either."

"Hate doing this on the phone," she paused, "but otherwise I'll never get to."

"What's that?"

"To tell you how much your friendship through high school meant to me, you watching over both GMag and me, especially after her surgery and through our senior year together. You knew my fear."

"Yeah, that your grandma might have problems, stuff left over from your mom's death."

"Right, but that didn't happen."

"God's in charge."

"Ian, you had to remind me of that so many times."

"I did."

"I am very grateful, for you being you."

"I know, hey I'll see you at the potluck."

Cassie made the plans, with Luke and Emma.

ℂ

"I'm so happy to see you guys, missed you all. Thank you for coming. We're good friends, forever?"

"Forever," she heard them in unison as they smiled and nodded to her.

Cassie saw the gladness in Luke's eyes. She looked around at her friends gathered at the outside table. They ate mounds of chicken, potato salad, and watermelon, lots of watermelon, and ice cream bars.

"Luke, it's been the longest for you."

"Yeah, to see all you, my old group."

He gazed at them, first Cassie, then Ian, then Emma.

"Can't believe it, but I'm a junior and I'm more sure than ever, it's gonna be medicine. What I'm not sure of, will it be the MD or will I want to get the PA. In health care now they're starting to turn to the Physician Assistant, a newer twist on helping out the docs so the MD's can specialize."

"Your folks?"

"Yeah, not gonna believe this, but they've each told me they're happy, in their own way. Dad's 'course, got no life from late fall through April 15. Guys, it's better for them."

Luke nodded as he looked at his friends.

"I drove by our old place; I'm staying with mom this weekend at her home. Anyway, a family, a couple of small bikes, were parked out in front. I'm glad that it's a family, like we were a family, times ago."

They remained silent, thinking about Luke and what had changed in his and their worlds. Cassie poured more lemonade as they commenced on their second helpings of food.

"Emma?"

She gave the group a broad smile, "Still got my HOPE."

They clapped together, "Congrats," she heard from her friends. "And I'm thinkin' I'm gonna follow the path of my grandparents."

"You'll teach?" Cassie asked.

"I think that's it, I'm lovin' the work I do with little first and second graders at the school where I volunteer. My advisor asked me to try the volunteer effort, that it might help me figure out where I'm headed. And I've met a nice guy, says he's headed to vet school after UGA."

She looked around at her friends. "He's serious about his studies, my friend first and foremost, and the first black guy I've ever really been around, you know, to get to know, since I've always lived with you guys, in your world."

"So spill, what'd he say when you told him you're black."

Emma nodded, "So predictable, he didn't believe me. Then I showed him our family picture, with my bro. Kinda stunned him to see how much I look like my mom."

"Ian?" Luke asked.

"So far, I'm makin' it on my HOPE and what my folks scrape together. I'm workin' maintenance days this summer like last and doin' a night auditor job at a hotel in downtown Ephrine. The night auditor gig, yeah, I know that's where I'm headed, to the accounting degree. And hey, now, in Georgia, I gotta get a masters in accounting before I can sit for the CPA. Cheez, I got no time for a woman."

"Huge bummer," Cassie said as she shook her head. Then she thought back to all their times together at Hillyer, hers and Ian's. "Thank you God, for Ian, for his incredible, close relationship with me, a true friendship."

"They expect a lot of people checkin' on the strength and weaknesses of people's bookkeeping."

"You're putting it nicely," Emma shook her head as she eyed Ian.

"So much corruption, out in the business world."

They all nodded to Ian.

"Hostess, we gotta hear, the lab scene."

"Uh huh, I worked my old ass off, got the grades, and I got picked up for a paid summer gig at a lab right there at UW in Madison. I'll head back for the fall in a week or so."

"Back in the dorm?"

She nodded.

"My summer assignment, water quality, oh my gosh, no idea what a big deal it is, for our water treatment plants all over the U.S."

She shook her head, "Anyway, us UW lab rats, we got broken down into groups, and mine worked on a water quality project in Africa, for Chad."

"Possible to help those folks, with their personal care habits, lack of toilets and sanitation?"

"Yeah Luke, it's possible to help them. There're volunteer groups, all over everywhere, and what they're teaching the folks is starting to work, at least in the area of Chad where UW is lending the what," Cassie paused, "the what they need is to clean up the water before they drink it."

"Sounds like Peace Corps work."

"Uh, huh, those folks help out too."

"Did you get to go to Africa, Cassie?"

"Nope, I was one of many of us who stayed back, doin' the analyses."

"How's that make you feel?"

"Small, there's so much stuff goin' on, so much work for microbiologists, for everybody in health, it's kinda overwhelming now."

Luke stayed on after Ian and Emma left. They continued to sit outside, having decaf coffee and the chocolate chip bars Cassie set aside for them. She made most of the recipe for her grandma, and a little bag for Luke to take back for his mom and him.

"Met anyone special yet, Cassie?"

"Nope, but I have three friends, all micro majors, and lab mates."

She felt his eyes on her and knew what he would ask her.

"One girl, two guys, yeah, I know before you even ask."

"You, Luke?"

"Several super girls, one pre-med, one in drama, so completely different from each other."

"Good."

He took her hand and directed his gaze to her.

"You're so entwined in my heart, with Annie, with our past, I will always love you, Cassie, my first wonderful love."

He watched tears glaze her eyes. She took her other hand and put it over Luke's.

"As you are, my first wonderful love, you'll be with me, always, forever."

7

Time passed for Cassie at her university

"Think you can handle it?"

Sam pierced her eyes with his gray green ones behind his glasses.

"Yeah, no prob, big boy, uh, Dr. Richards, let's head over to the facility."

Cassie looked over to her dark-haired friend and touched his shoulder as he drove his squeaky old Volvo station wagon for the visit. She peered out the window noticing the sky darken as they arrived. Her mind spiraled back to her second microbiology class as a sophomore.

Sam stood with the professor in front of the assembled students. She felt completely gobsmacked that first time she saw him, tall, built, with dark brown horn-rimmed glasses. He pretty much ended up co-teaching the class that semester as the prof got sicker and sicker. Sam couldn't help but notice her. Cassie pulled the top grade on every test, paper, and quiz. He graded them all. Toward the end of the semester he decided to introduce himself. He had to meet her.

When he finally did, "All of this, in one package," was his thought.

She remembered that he spoke to her of her brilliance, and he told her how beautiful she was. And that he wouldn't date someone in a class with which he was assisting. He explained the completion of his doctorate in microbiology and where he thought he headed. That was a year and a half ago.

Cassie's mind returned to the task at hand, the visit. They held hands as they walked into the reception area leading to individual rooms in the AIDS wing. He squeezed her hand and let go. They separated. Cassie walked along with the kindly white-haired woman who spoke in soft whispers as she explained. She saw room after room, sick young man after sick young man. After she viewed 10 of the sick folks, she asked if she could sit down for a couple of minutes.

"I thought I'd handle this better, but I'm just so sad," she told her guide.

"God's children, we're all God's children."

She put her head in her hands as she remembered what she just saw. They were once beautiful young people, just like her and Sam, right now. Many of them had purple plaque all over their faces, arms, chests, legs. That horrible look meant cancer of the blood vessels, named Kaposi sarcoma. But what was worse was what she heard, gasping, gasping for every breath that their withered bodies took. The fungus inside the young men's lungs, pneumocystis pneumonia, called PCP.

"Find a cure, find a way to help."

Cassie heard those words in the classrooms, in the labs, in 1995, her first fall semester at UW. At the end of the year the stats came in, for all of them in the sciences, over 43,000 deaths due to AIDS. And here she was looking at what that was, devastating to young people, some her own age.

She felt sick, a beating headache, with her every heartbeat. And her lungs, from hearing the death rattles in the rooms, her lungs ached. She tried to take shallow breaths, but it didn't help.

Sam thanked the AIDS helpers. Cassie tried to move along at a good pace, but her legs didn't want to carry her. Once they got outside she headed to bushes and puked, again and again. Sam held her upright until they got to the car. She leaned against it and began to cry.

"That's gotta be one of the most horrible, most horrible."

Sam held her close and as she quieted he spoke out.

"Do you see, understand, the concern for all of us in the health fields, this is a disaster happening."

"I understand."

"Cassie, I know you got more to say."

"Everyone's working on the cure, the meds to make this situation better, here, and all over the rest of the world, right?"

"That's right, so many folks working."

"Sam, God's in charge, do you think God's trying to tell these young people something, maybe about the way they love each other, that way seems to be contributing to this whole mess."

"Yeah, you may be right; wrath's unleashed on these kids."

"You know what?"

"What?"

"I got a paid position, internship, for the summer, in Atlanta, with the National Center, the one working on HIV, STD's, and unbelievable still TB."

She stood back from Sam, shaking her head.

"Yeah, I know, we've still got tuberculosis out there."

They drove back to her dorm, and he walked with her into the reception area.

"I'm feeling better; please sit with me for a minute."

They sat together at a loveseat.

"It came up, in of all places, in my virology class. The students got so worked up, shouting out, not understanding the stupidity of people."

"OK, what's the fuss?"

"HIV in babies, can you believe it, now the little ones're getting sick, from their mom's who've got HIV and AIDS."

"And the argument?"

"Wearing condoms when having sex."

"Yeah, it's what we're all supposed to do, the condom protects against the virus, protects somewhat."

"Uh huh, better than nothing."

They sat in silence for a while.

"I can't understand, Sam, that a couple can't take a moment from their ecstasy to do something to protect themselves."

"Maybe they don't care."

"Sam, that must be it; they'll put their lives on the line. But when she ends up pregnant, it's just not fair if the baby's HIV too."

He hugged her, "We're all working hard, in our own research, the whole community of health and medicine, all over the world, to try to ease this tragedy."

"I know I shouldn't get so worked up; we lose some 20,000 folks every year from the stupid old flu."

"Uh huh, we do have the flu shot."

"Right, it helps."

"But stuff for AIDS, we're still exploratory."

"That's for sure."

℥

The summer of 1998 Cassie lived in a dorm at Georgia Tech, a new facility that Tech got after the 1996 Summer Olympics happened in Atlanta. She spent long hours at the Institute.

"I'm doin' what I love, searchin', researchin', looking for answers, working on what it will take to break this virus."

She spoke that with everyone she worked with, and with the couple of friends she made during the short time she lived in Atlanta. Sam wanted to meet her grandma. At the end of her internship, she returned to Ephrine for a short visit before returning to Wisconsin for her last semester.

Sam flew in to Atlanta and drove to Ephrine in a rental car.

"GMag, meet Dr. Sam Richards."

Maggie looked up into this tall man's grayish green eyes and smiled.

"Welcome," she gave him a firm handshake.

She moved her eyes to Cassie and gave her a nod, of approval.

Cassie returned her grandma's nod with a wide smile.

"This's a celebration of Thanksgiving, you two, because only the Lord knows where exactly you all will be in November."

The ham, Maggie baked the ham she always fixed for the Thanksgiving potluck. Cassie whipped up the pumpkin pie and salad. They gave Sam the job of baking the rolls for the meal. They ate and ate.

"Actually I'm a pretty darn good cook. I've got an appetite, and my mom made me help with the meals growin' up. I'm super glad of that now," he chuckled.

"Well, you're cleaning the chow up in double quick fashion. Cassie, how many pies did you bake?"

They laughed together as she shook her head and held up one finger.

"That'll do," Sam nodded

They took their pie and decaf coffee to the couch in the great room. Cassie looked about the room, remembering so many occasions she had, eating and conversing in this very room.

Sam directed his gaze to Maggie.

"I love Cassie."

Cassie turned to her grandma, "And I love Sam."

Maggie held her hands together and smiled to them both.

"God bless and keep you."

"We got so much going on in our lives, right now, moving on."

"Cassie will graduate in December."

"And, GMag, I've applied for a position, at the CDC, but it might not end up being in Atlanta."

"And I'm into month three of a project, off site, for the University of Wisconsin. It's what I want, Cassie knows."

He nodded first to Cassie and then to Maggie.

They finished their pie. Sam returned with a second piece and poured them more decaf coffee.

"And we have, maybe I shouldn't even say," Cassie stopped.

"I'm medical, you two, and I know you're into the whole HIV/AIDS situation, well I call it an epidemic, world-wide I'm reading that now there are over 13 million children under 15 who are AIDS orphans, missing parents, that's just grotesque."

"But we do have news," Cassie stopped and nodded her head, "a glimmer of hope in this whole terrible mess."

"That is?"

"Antiretroviral therapy."

"Really, happening now?"

Sam nodded, "And there are stats to back up some success, the death rate's down to 13,000 a year in the US."

"Oh my goodness, you two, well Cassie, we've talked several years back, uh about, what was it, 43,000, your freshman year?"

"Wow, GMag, you've got a phenome memory. Yeah," she looked to Sam and smiled, "maybe some hope?"

Sam nodded to her.

"Still think we got many years to go before we've a handle on this, develop better therapies, and learn more about the microorganisms and viruses that cause diseases."

"Sounds like you two are out in the trenches, open warfare, against what's going on."

Cassie looked at her grandma, "Soldiers, we're soldiers, in this struggle. Wow, like Dad and I talked, after mom died, when we knew what had to happen. We came out of the shadows of our grieving lives, into sunshine, more positive happening for us. And that's the way it's been through the past years."

"Glimmers of hope, for those sick ones still with us," Sam added.

"Maybe, from shadow to more sunshine in some of their lives."

Maggie nodded to them, "My sincerest hope, for you two, and for all of us, to go on to a life of discovery, and lives together, with love."

TOGETHER NOW

Book 3 in the *Jenny / Ann Trilogy*

14-year-old Emily cherishes her long-time friendships with Coop, Kate, Nate, and Pete. These high school sophomores enjoy the time they spend together writing plays, composing music and creating lyrics as 5 group. Best friends, Emily and Kate, plan their future dreams, Emily in engineering and Kate in drama. At the Fall Festival they perform their own musical, *The Princess and her Dragon*. The success of the play encourages them to expand their drama efforts.

5 group hate losing Pete, who is forced to move away. All of them participate in a community theater production as 4 group. Understudies, Coop and Kate, take the lead roles when illness strikes two main characters. Sexual temptation and alcohol overtake the four of them after they celebrate the play's completion. Emily begins a friendship with Ethan and that summer works in the office of a construction company, moving her closer to her engineering dream. After months of being apart, 4 group come together as singers at an outside church Christmas program.

Both Emily and Kate lose parents, Kate's dad and Emily's mom. 5 group (with Pete back) gather after they all graduate from college and share their jobs, schooling and future plans. Emily acknowledges her nagging doubt about her mom (Ann). She finds a diary hidden in a dress in her mom's closet. While reading the diary Emily learns about her mom's past. Together Now is the final book of the *Jenny/Ann Trilogy* including *Christmas Bright* and *Baskets on Christmas Lane*.

ABOUT CATHLEEN

Cathleen Ellis is a Colorado native. She and her husband, John, live in the northern part of the state. They have four sons, three daughters-in-law, and four grandchildren. Cathleen draws the inspiration for her love stories from the lives of young people with whom she has lived and worked her entire life.

WWW.CATHLEENELLIS.COM